Dark Motives

by

Dianne McCartney

The Elijah Black Trilogy, Book 2

Dark Motives

Cover Art by *Kim Mendoza*

The Wild Rose Press, Inc.
PO Box 708
Adams Basin, NY 14410-0708
Visit us at www.thewildrosepress.com

Publishing History
First Edition, 2022
Trade Paperback ISBN 978-1-5092-4150-7
Digital ISBN 978-1-5092-4151-4

The Elijah Black Trilogy, Book 2
Published in the United States of America

Dedication

This book is dedicated to the police officers who keep the peace in challenging times.

And, as always, to my husband, Mitch, daughter, Colleen and son-in-law, John.

Chapter One

Detective Alvia Sanchez waited in the car, as she often did on Friday mornings, for Elijah to place his rose on Cara's grave and return.

The irreverent side of her wanted to tell him the weekly visits were overkill, but she kept her mouth zipped. Each to his own. She would never understand his connection to a serial killer. At least her partner had returned from the depths of despair, even though he wasn't yet powering at full throttle.

He finally returned, folding his long legs and climbing behind the wheel. She paused as he started the car, then handed him a donut. Shrugging, he ate it as he wound through the endless lines of gravestones to the ornate, black iron front gate. It was a sign of the times that his usual healthy food choices had taken a temporary back seat to her far less prudent offerings.

After arriving at their precinct, they were hailed at the top of the stairs by Detective Albert Jones. Brown-haired, brown-eyed, and remarkably average in every way, he never stood out, but was, at least, reliable. Even his shirt was a bland, beige color as though color had abandoned the cause. "Boss wants to see you both pronto," he said, a smirk twisting his pale face.

Thanking him, they diverted down the long hall to Lieutenant Allen Porter's office. He looked distracted, as always. With the day barely begun, his restless hands had already disturbed his graying hair. "Sit down," he said, gesturing at the timeworn chairs across the desk from his own. "We just caught a murder uptown. Sylvia Bennett, owner of a string of five-star restaurants, was found shot to death in her apartment. She's a socialite, very high profile, plastered all over social media. I need you two to handle this one."

"Yes, sir," Elijah said. "Are there other detectives on scene?"

"Hadley and Davis are holding it for you. They're overseeing the evidence team and managing crowd control. Someone from the medical examiner's office should have arrived by the time you get there. They're still short-handed."

Elijah knew Hadley in particular wouldn't be happy at him and Sanchez taking point on this case or any other. He typically made being unsatisfied a full-time occupation. "Anything else, sir?"

Their boss gave a pronounced sigh. "I hope I'm wrong, but from what I've been told, it feels like a symbolic killing which might mean the killer's not done. I hope you make my workday easier by proving me wrong." He pushed a square of colored paper with the address scrawled on it across the desk. "Keep me informed."

"Yes, sir."

They fought their way through what remained of the morning's rush hour traffic to an elegant high rise uptown. A sizable crowd had already gathered outside, undeterred by the cool autumn air. New York news hounds were a ravenous bunch, chomping on the fetid meat of murder. Leaving their car parked near the entrance brought a scowl to the stalwart doorman's face until they held up their credentials. He nodded and waved them inside, holding back the group of milling reporters who shoved too close to the door. Their shouted questions sounded muffled from the interior.

"Tenth floor," Elijah said to Sanchez, nodding at the cop stationed in the downstairs hall as they walked past. Entering the elevator, they waited as the gleaming doors closed and the snug metal box lifted them upwards. On their arrival, they counted six spacious apartments on the floor, three on each side. The only thing that bought you so much space in this city was a veritable hoard of money. They headed for the one unit in the far corner. Sounds of activity beckoned them through the open door into the carnage beyond.

Detective Barry "Bear" Davis looked up and nodded a greeting, his smile reaching his expressive blue eyes. He'd once been a champion linebacker in university until a knee injury forced him out of a promising future in football. His sheer brawn was enough to intimidate most criminals. A pleasant, easygoing guy, he was well-liked by everyone, especially the ladies who were drawn to both his broad shoulders and his thick, golden hair.

His partner, Phil Hadley, was another story. He saw them coming and crossed his arms, a familiar snarky expression compressing his face. Considered a snappy dresser, at least by himself, his mud-colored hair was coiffed so that his bangs lifted off his thin, pinched forehead.

Davis moved beside Elijah, knowing he and Hadley didn't get along. "Hey, you two. We've got a forty-two-year-old female, Sylvia Bennett, dead from three bullet wounds. Doc's with her now, so we should have time of death in a minute."

"No witnesses?"

"Two of the guys just started canvassing the neighbors. Haven't heard anything yet."

"Who found her?"

"The housekeeper." He pointed through a doorway to the nearby bedroom where a small, dark-haired woman sat in a chair, sobbing. Framed by the opening, she appeared as if posed for a painting titled Sorrow, her tear-stained face the very definition of melancholy.

"Can you take care of her?" he asked Sanchez. Nodding, she moved over to the other woman and crouched down beside her. Clasping one of her hands, she spoke softly in Spanish. For all of her brashness, she had an uncanny way with witnesses that proved invaluable.

Elijah always proved more adept with the presentation of the crime itself and the picture the killer left behind. He wished they had been the first ones to arrive on scene. First impressions, unsullied by the presence of others, were always helpful. Starting toward the body, he was thwarted by Hadley stepping in front of him, his legs braced and his hands dangling at each side, curled into fists. "Busy grabbing everyone's cases these days, aren't you, boy wonder? Wouldn't want anyone else's name smeared all over the front page."

His jaw set, he met the other man's accusing gaze. Territorial issues caused by an overblown ego wasted valuable time better spent on investigation. "I go wherever my lieutenant requires me to assist. If you have a problem with that, I suggest you take your complaints up with him."

Swearing under his breath, the other man stormed off, stomping his feet like a rebellious child. His renowned temper would get him fired one day, but it hadn't happened yet. Davis shrugged, waved goodbye, and followed Hadley out the door. It was a good thing Davis could put up with his partner because no one else seemed interested in such an exhausting job.

Elijah approached Dr. Stanford Hayes as the medical examiner straightened. "Good morning, doc. I thought your assistant would be here."

"Which assistant? The latest one just quit. Not many can stand up to the workload." The tall, gray-haired man tightened his lips to a flat line. "Your lieutenant asked me to take a look because of the specific nature of the injuries." He gestured toward the body and stood aside so Elijah could take a gander.

One glance told the story and had him cringing. The oozing wounds were in each of the woman's breasts and in between her legs, the blood an indelible red marker on her clothes. "I see what you mean. It's a statement of sorts as if he's attacking women in general. That makes me worry she won't be the last."

"She's been dead around ten hours, so say ten-thirty to eleven last night. The wound near the heart was likely the fatal one. Beyond that supposition, we'll have to see what the autopsy tells us." He sighed, stretching his neck from side to side as a crackling sound accompanied his movements. "The evidence team has already finished with her. Take all the time you need, then I'll release the body to the attendants."

The attractive woman wore a stylish blue suit, her long, dark hair puddled in a shining mass on her shoulder. Matching heels looked as if they'd been kicked off in one corner of the room. Expensive diamond earrings glittered from her ear lobes. Her jewelry was untouched, and a small stack of cash lay in a tray on the glass coffee table. No one had been looking to make money off this kill. The assailant came with a singular purpose in mind.

The wounds hadn't bled much which meant that her heart stopped beating quickly. Neither he nor Sanchez could determine anything out of the ordinary. There wasn't anything more to see as far as the victim herself was concerned. He thanked Dr. Hayes and let them remove the body.

A sleek, leather briefcase sat on the polished mahogany coffee table along with a silver laptop. Walking around to take a look, he noticed it was open to a popular dating site. He turned to call for Sanchez, only to find her standing at his side. "Can you figure out what she was looking at on that site before she died?"

"Sure thing." She sat, and he watched, impressed, as her gloved fingers zipped over the keys. "She's had a profile posted here for the last six months. Lots of interested guys, not a surprise. She was a beautiful woman."

"Anything refer to any plans for last night?"

"Yup. By the sound of the messages, she met an accountant named David Petrie at Interludes in uptown last night. It's a really nice, new restaurant. Expensive."

Nodding, he scrawled the information in his tattered notebook. "Did you find anything in the bedrooms?"

"Nah. Both master and guest room beds are made, and nothing looked disturbed." They went back together for a second look to be certain they hadn't missed anything. He agreed with his partner, though. The bedrooms looked untouched.

He led her back to the living room. "Okay. It appears as if the victim relaxed on the sofa, searching the site. Then she heard something and was moving toward the sound when he shot her." He glanced at his watch. "I don't think there's much left for us to see here. Her housekeeper tell you anything useful?"

"She arrives at the same time every weekday morning. Today, she opened the door with her key, saw her body, screamed, and ran out to the hall to call 911. Poor bitch, she'll have nightmares for years." Sighing, she said, "She said Bennet was in a good mood yesterday, looking forward to her date."

"So, not much helpful there."

"She did tell me something interesting, though. She said our victim used to occasionally leave the door unlocked even though she warned her against it. And she never bothered to use the peephole. Bennett had ultimate faith in the doorman and her neighbors."

"So, probably, our killer saw her do it and knew he could access the interior if he just waited long enough."

"Or she knew her killer and let him in."

"True." He waved for her to follow. "Let's leave the team to finish. Time to find out where David Petrie works and see what he has to say about last night."

As usual, he drove while his partner combed the Internet on her phone. A little digging showed Petrie had his own small accounting firm downtown. He and Sanchez tracked down the neat, brick building, sandwiched between a clothing store and a delicatessen, in twenty minutes. Lucky to find a nearby parking spot, they entered to find a pleasant older woman at the tidy reception desk, filing her nails. Her welcoming smile dimmed at the sight of their badges, a reaction to which they'd become accustomed. She cleared her throat. Instead of the usual may I help you, she asked, "Is anything wrong?"

"We'd like to have a word with Mr. Petrie. Is he in?"

"Yes. I'll get him." Rather than calling him on the telephone, she excused herself, standing and hustling down the brightly lit hall, out of sight. In a few moments, a tall, blond man came striding out, pulling off a pair of dark framed glasses. He lived on the handsome side of nerddom. A palpable look of concern on his face spoke of the paranoia their visits often caused.

"How can I help you, officers?"

They introduced themselves, showing their badges. Elijah shook his hand. "Could we have a word in private, please?"

"Of course." Ignoring the receptionist's curious, concerned expression, he led the way to a large, utilitarian office, decorated in simple cream and brown. Besides one rather uninspiring painting, only his degrees in plain black frames hung on the wall. Three modern chairs and a plain oak desk were the only furniture. "Have a seat." Unbuttoning the button on his suit coat, he took the chair behind his desk and waited for them to speak.

Elijah waited for Sanchez to settle in her chair, then turned to him. "Are you acquainted with a woman named Sylvia Bennett?"

A puzzled expression crossed his face. "Yes. We

just met. We had a lovely dinner last night." His face paled as he made the uncomfortable connection between their jobs and her. "Is something wrong with Sylvia?"

He looked to Sanchez as if searching for reassurance. She leaned forward, meeting his gaze. "I'm afraid Ms. Bennett was murdered last night."

"M-murdered?" His hands shook, and he lowered them to the surface of his desk, one clasping the other in an obvious attempt at comfort. His shocked gaze met hers. "I don't understand. How? Who would do such a terrible thing?"

"We were hoping you could provide us with some details about last night," she said, softening her tone. "Can you tell me what time your date started and ended?"

"I booked our reservation for seven-thirty, and we remained there until around ten. After that, I helped her hail a cab in front of the restaurant, saw her inside, then headed home. I live a short distance away, so I walked." He presented the information in a robotic manner, his eyes glazed. After a moment's consideration, he gave them the name of the taxi company.

Sanchez scrawled the information in her notepad. "Did you notice anyone paying particular attention to her either in the restaurant or near the cab?"

"No, but I wasn't really paying attention to anyone else. I found her quite charming." He wiped his hand across his face, fingers trembling. "It seemed, you know, normal. Just a regular first date."

"And what was your impression of Ms. Bennett?"

"She was really pretty. Confident, but a little shy.

She said during our online discussions she found most men too forward, that their assumptions about sexual availability made her uncomfortable." He dredged up a smile. "She would have been perfect for me, because I like to take my time getting to know someone." Leaning back, he lay a hand on his stomach and rubbed. "Oh, this is awful."

"During the evening, did she happen to mention any issues she was having with other men? Anyone being too persistent or any unexpected gifts that were sent to her?"

"I'm afraid not. She just made that one general comment about men being too forward. I think she told me that so I wouldn't make the same mistake." He shook his head. "She needn't have worried. That's just not my style." Looking up, he asked, "Where did she die?"

"In her apartment."

He heaved in a breath. "I wish I'd seen her to her door. I offered, but she didn't want me to, and I respected her choice. Now I wish I had. My presence might have scared him off."

Sanchez reached over to lay her hand on his. "You aren't in any way responsible. He was likely lying in wait inside her apartment. Seeing her to the door wouldn't have changed the eventual outcome."

Elijah asked, "Were you planning to call her again?"

The other man met his gaze, signaling profound regret. "Yes. I planned to call her today and ask if she'd like to go out with me a second time. Our dinner together was the most enjoyable date I've had in years."

His words touched Elijah. The dating world in New

York was challenging at best. His partner lay one of her business cards on his desk. "If you think of anything else, no matter how minor it might seem, please give us a call."

As they were escorted out by the receptionist, they left him slumped in his office chair, staring at the blotter as if to block out their conversation. His receptionist, looking concerned, waited for an explanation with her eyebrows raised. When none was forthcoming, she saw them to the door briskly as if anxious to be rid of them. They took the elevator down in silence because some other occupants shared the car. Once back down on the street and out of earshot, she said, "It's not him."

Elijah agreed. "Just another nice guy trying to find his person. I can identify with that. We'll check out his timeframe anyway, but I think it'll back him up."

Their next stop was at the elegant restaurant where the two had met. Interludes had lunch and dinner hours. They arrived a few minutes before eleven and watched from outside as the staff opened up the place, unlocking the door and swishing the floor-length curtains open. Stepping inside, they scanned the shining ebony tables surrounded by ivory upholstered chairs. Elegant gold-framed mirrors bounced the light around the room.

Once summoned, the helpful female manager listened to their request and led them to a back room where the equipment for the security cameras was kept. With her permission, Sanchez took over and wound the recording back to the time of the arrival of their subjects. The manager allowed them to do their job and stood back to watch, twitching with interest.

Petrie arrived a few minutes before his date,

dressed in a pristine navy suit, white shirt, and burgundy tie. He was seated by the hostess and sat, fiddling with obvious nerves, until his date showed up. His face beamed with both relief and pleasure at her approach. Her stylish blue suit was both pretty and demure. After the first few moments, they seemed quite at ease with each other with no sign of any discomfort on either side. Conversation flowed. The meal looked delicious, and they both appeared to enjoy it, taking their time. A few minutes before ten, they left together. The camera near the front entrance showed the couple through the glass as he handed her into a cab. He stood on the curb and waited until the cab drove away to begin his walk home.

The cameras told the story, and he wished that happened more often. It would make substantiating alibis so much easier. They spoke to the young waitress who'd served the couple, but she didn't have anything else to add. She pronounced both customers as 'nice' and said Petrie had tipped better than average at twenty percent. They took the security disc with them with the owner's consent.

Neither uttered a word until they were inside the car. "Technically, he could have circled back and surprised her at home." Sanchez, always the devil's advocate, dug in her oversized purse for a candy bar.

"Did he strike you as the type to kill her?"

"Nah. Just the opposite. You?"

"I agree. We'll check into him more to cover our bases, but he's not our guy. Besides, he would have had to be in place to ambush her, and there simply wasn't enough time to beat her to her place. I would bet that security recordings will bear that out."

They headed back to the precinct and updated their boss. Further investigations showed Petrie returning to his apartment and never leaving again that night. As they expected, the data on the security cameras of his own building and surrounding buildings proved it.

They tracked down the cab driver who had driven Bennett home and verified that she had made no unexpected stops along the way. That bit of information cleared Petrie of any wrongdoing as they'd expected.

Back to square one. It would have been nice to have an easy solution that solved the case, but it rarely happened that way. Only in domestic cases was the first suspect often the killer.

The two of them spent arduous hours going through the substantial amount of information on Bennett's life. She had a thriving social media presence, mostly centered on her travels, food, and fashion. They couldn't locate any threatening emails or something that set off alarm bells. The desk calendar they'd found in her office attested to numerous first-time dates, but few follow-ups. At midnight, they gave up and went home to grab a few hours' sleep.

Chapter Two

Early the next morning, Elijah landed at his desk, yawning as he took his seat. No matter how hard he tried, he couldn't make three hours sleep truly restful. A few minutes after he started working, Detective Jones stuck his head into the open doorway. "See the newspaper this morning?"

He looked up. "Haven't had a chance yet. Why? Something I need to see?"

Taking a few steps in, the other man threw a folded copy on his desk. "Looks like your boy wants to play." With those teasing words, he disappeared down the corridor.

Unfolding the paper, Elijah read the headline that topped the front page. "Is Taunting Rhyme from a Serial Killer?" Below was a poem of sorts that had apparently been sent to the newsroom.

Sylvia Bennett
She should have stayed in the kitchen where she belongs
Instead of acting the boss, as a woman that's wrong
I know how to put those types in their place
Stay there or meet destiny face to face
Signed
"The Rhymester"

"Ah, hell," he muttered. Knowing the killer had just given the press a name to smear all over the headlines peeved him. The careless act of a serial killer assuming a special name just increased their sense of self-importance, the very last thing they needed. As he started down the hall to talk to the lieutenant, his phone buzzed. Since he saw it was his boss calling, he waited until he stepped inside the office door. "I didn't answer because I was almost here."

Porter sighed, leaning back in his chair to fold his arms over his chest. "In cases like this, I hate when my instincts are right."

"I understand how you feel."

"Nothing helpful showed up last night?"

"No, sir. Sanchez and I worked until midnight. The man Bennett had the date with, Petrie, is squeaky clean. Numerous security cameras confirmed his whereabouts. Bennett returned alone, but the security cameras at her residence were jammed for about forty minutes before she arrived and twenty minutes afterwards. That matches her approximate time of death and would cover him coming and going. And, so far, the neighbors have been no help. No one saw or heard anything."

"Do we know how he gained access yet?"

"Not yet, but apparently she was sloppy with security. She didn't always lock her door and never checked her peephole, according to her housekeeper."

"So he either took advantage of her habits or he knew her."

"Yes, sir."

"If he managed to thwart the security cameras, he has better than average computer skills."

"So does Sanchez, sir. She said the signals from certain security systems can be jammed with a simple device you can order on the Internet."

"That's true. Or so I've heard." He raised his eyebrows. "That's neither my forte nor yours, right?"

"Yes. I'm thankful to have her for more reasons than I can count, but her particular skill in that area is priceless."

He tapped a pencil on his desk. "We have a news conference on this case this afternoon. I'd like to have Sanchez stand beside you."

"Just between you and me, sir, she won't be glad to hear that."

He chuckled. "I understand it's not her favorite thing. With the misogynist bent this case demonstrates, I think we need to stress a successful man/woman partnership. It might rattle him."

"That makes sense. We'll take all the help we can get. I'll tell her."

"You still need to answer the questions which should keep her happy. The picture of you two working together is a visual this department needs, considering the current political climate. A way to showcase the men and women in blue, working together, in a way that benefits both."

"I see your point."

"Three o'clock in the media room."

"Yes, sir. We'll be there."

He returned to find Sanchez sprawled behind her desk and filled her in on the request for her presence at the press briefing. Standing, she swore at him in Spanish and threw her stress ball at his head.

Ducking, he laughed as it glanced off the wall behind him. The words meant nothing to him, and she knew it. "Not my idea, I promise you."

"I hate that shit. Why in hell would he make me do

that?"

"He wants to demonstrate the value of both men and women being on the force. Especially with this particular case."

"What kind of bullshit am I supposed to spout?" Her hands waved in the air like a bird flapping his wings, accenting her words.

He grinned. "Now comes the good news. You don't have to say anything. I'll just refer to you as my trusted, longtime partner, and all you have to do is look noble."

"Noble, eh… What, like a dog?"

"I like dogs."

Another string of curses preceded her dropping into her chair with a thump. "Jerk."

Smothering a laugh, he got back to work. They spent the two hours after lunch interviewing the victim's distraught sister who had nothing helpful to add. She could barely speak between bouts of weeping. Sadly, there were no other family members left to console her.

The dating site had provided a few more names they would look into, but only to cover their bases. None of the men looked especially worrisome from a cursory check, but face-to-face interviews would help cement their impressions.

At two-thirty, he took a few minutes to coach his partner about the news conference, persuading her to tidy her bank of wild girl hair. For the first time in his memory, she seemed nervous, standing periodically to pace back and forth. "Give them calm and confident. This dog and pony show is just to show them we're on the hunt."

She kept her mouth zipped on the walk over, hurrying to keep pace with his longer stride. Once in the crowded media room, she stayed glued to his side, saying as little as possible to the commissioner and mayor after greeting them. As usual, those two men did the introductions and covered the basic facts of the case thus far. Afterwards, he and Sanchez were introduced, and they stepped up to the microphone. Elijah could feel his partner tremble, an unusual thing.

He fielded the expected questions:

How long have you two been partners?

Does she do all the paperwork?

The second one made him angry, and he fought to temper his response. "Both men and women are expected to perform all required duties, both in the office and in the field. It's an insult to every woman in the department to insinuate anything else. Detective Sanchez has superior skills to my own in computer work. Hopefully, someday, I'll catch up. Next question."

"Are you a couple?"

They'd been asked this earlier this year. "No. We are friends and effective working partners." He chose a reliable reporter in the hopes of a more intelligent question. Pamela Clayton had been on the crime beat for several years. Her flamboyant blonde appearance hid a canny mind, despite the fact that others often called her the name of a famous fashion doll behind her back.

"Is this crime more about successful working women in general rather than Ms. Bennett personally?"

"We are looking into that possibility because of the poem sent to one of our local newspapers." He chose the man next to her.

"Do you anticipate more murders in the near future?"

"Commenting on possible future outcomes would be irresponsible. Thank you. That's all for today."

They filed out, ignoring the shouted questions which echoed behind them. He and Sanchez slipped down a back hall to escape the pursuing crowd.

****

The Rhymester stared at the television, anger tensing all of his muscles. Rage made him gulp for air, only to have it rush back out again. A flush of anger heated his cheeks. The little Hispanic bitch sashayed up on stage as if she had every right to be there.

In the old days, she would have been kicked out the police academy on height restrictions alone. She was a joke, taking the place of a hard-working man who should be standing there instead of her. And the oh-so-honorable Detective Black didn't help, bragging about his partner's supposed contributions to the case. That took his brown-nosing to a whole new level.

He already had his next two victims planned, but she could still be added to the lineup. No one would ever catch him. Observing the people who tried was like watching that vintage television show about cops chasing each other around like rabid mice. Yeah, picking off the police department's new poster girl would give him a little added glee somewhere down the line.

And his list of targets just kept growing.

****

After the news conference, Sanchez flopped into her worn chair, a gusty sigh bursting forth. "How do you do it?"

"Do what?" he replied, although he knew what she meant.

"All that ass kissin'. I mean, seriously, doesn't it get old?"

"Yes, it does. I don't mind the serious questions, but the thoughtless ones drive me up the wall."

She bared her teeth like a cornered wolverine. "If you expected me to do your paperwork, I'd tell you to put it where the sun don't shine."

He grinned across at her. "And so, you should."

"I was going to go through Bennett's financials next."

"Sounds good. Why don't I do the interviews with the other three men she dated recently? I don't have high hopes, but at least we can strike them off the list."

Two of those men could drop by the precinct that afternoon. He made an appointment to go to the third man's office the following morning. By the end of the day, he suffered a pounding headache. Both lengthy interviews had yielded nothing, but two perfectly normal men who appeared horrified at the news. They both had solid alibis which he'd checked out immediately after they left the building.

Personally, he couldn't imagine meeting someone he wanted to date online. Searching his memory, he could remember at least seven murders he'd heard of which had started with individuals meeting in that manner. That information convinced him to steer clear. But who was he to talk? The last date he'd had, she'd turned out to be a serial killer. He shoved Cara Belton from his mind.

Some days, it was hard to remember people of

good character still existed in the world. Cops, surrounded daily by crime, death, and politics, often struggled to remember that. The latter was a tortured dance which became more tiresome every day.

In the meantime, he had to focus on finding a man who wanted to taunt and play games. Those type of killers were the worst. Because no matter what he told the press, he knew there'd be another body. With the current lack of evidence, he also knew they had zero chance of stopping him in time.

****

Sanchez rolled home just before ten, dragging through the door of her apartment with a tired sigh.

"Hey, sugar." Her boyfriend, Ray's, voice reached her from somewhere inside. "I'm in the kitchen."

She kicked off her shoes, letting them bang against the wall with a satisfying thud. Padding into the kitchen, she raised her face in his direction for a kiss. Eight inches taller than her, he bent to give her a resounding smack on the lips. Not satisfied with one, he lifted her up onto her toes and kissed her senseless. Why do Italian guys always have such great hair, she thought, as she ran her hands through the dark waves. He stepped back, his chocolate eyes twinkling at her enthusiastic response.

She pulled out of his arms. "What, you drink too many energy drinks again?"

"Nah, I just missed you." Wandering to the stove, he grabbed a wooden spoon and stirred. "Sit down. I made you some pasta."

Sniffing the delicious aromas of garlic and tomato, she hummed in appreciation. Sometimes she felt guilty about how attentive he was compared to her. "Good.

I'm starvin'." Yawning, she asked, "How was work?"

"Same old, same old."

He'd been on the force once, years ago, but was now head of hotel security at a fancy hotel downtown. They'd met there in the middle of the first Belton murder scene, a diehard cop's version of the height of romance. "I could have changed places with you today."

He piled the pasta on her plate and, turning, smiled. "I saw you on television. You and Elijah, looking like cop royalty. The boys and babes in blue."

"Good thing he does all the talkin'. I probably would have just said, 'What a pile of dog crap' and walked off the stage."

"Why did they make you get up there? They usually don't."

"They're sending this killer a message. He's a miso—you know. He hates women."

"Misogynist." He set the plate down with a fork, shook a shower of parmesan to cover the top, and stepped back as she dug in with gusto.

"Yeah, that." She chewed the food enough to talk around it. "Anyway, it's the whole united front thing, I guess."

"You guys come up with any way to stop him?"

"I hate to be negative, but not a chance in hell at this point. And we probably don't have much time before his next kill if he's already blabbin' to the press."

"You can only do so much, babe."

"I know. Now I just have to convince Elijah."

He glanced at his watch. "Mind if I spend the night?"

She rolled her eyes. "You think you're so sneaky. I already saw that you stuck your overnight bag in the front closet."

Smiling, he shrugged. "You wouldn't kick your man out, would you? Especially not after he made you a nice dinner."

She probably should, just to prove she could make herself do it, but she didn't have the heart. Or any real inclination for that matter. Her relying on him too much was a worry for another day. "You want some lovin', you're gonna have to do the heavy liftin' and make it worth my while. I'm beat."

"Oh, I think I'm up to the challenge." He started across the kitchen toward her.

****

The next morning, Lieutenant Porter gestured Elijah through the doorway. "Remember the Green case a few months ago. Guy killed his wife with a screwdriver? You and Sanchez took care of it, right?"

"Yes, sir."

He frowned. "It just got kicked to the new assistant D.A. and she has concerns."

Taking a seat, he asked, "What kind of concerns?"

"Apparently, the psychiatrist who certified him as competent lied about his credentials. All of his cases are being looked at again."

"Wonderful. Just what we need right now."

"I agree. Do you think you can spare a few minutes to go down to talk to her? Let's find out how to address her concerns and help get the prosecution of this case back on track."

"What's her name? We met briefly when she arrived, but I'm afraid I've forgotten."

"Dayle Stockard. Transferred in from Texas. Graduated at the top of her class and is considered brilliant. Whether we agree or not remains to be seen."

"Thank you. I'll let you know how it goes."

As he walked to the nearby building where her office was located, he struggled to remember if he was thinking of the right person. The dormant memory popped up with surprising clarity; a tall, brunette woman with dark eyes that dissected you. It was a passing thought, based on a thirty-second introduction. They'd had other assistant DAs who had worked well with the police and a few that hadn't. It remained to be seen which group she would fall into—he hoped the former. It would make life much easier for everyone concerned.

He travelled up to the bustling fourth floor on an elevator packed with people, hoping this wouldn't take long. When he poked his head into her office, it was empty. Since ten a.m. had come and gone, surely she'd be in the office by now even if she'd had a late night.

"May I help you?"

The cool tone held a hint of suspicion. Turning, he saw the object of his search waiting behind him, a mug of steaming coffee in her hand. "Good morning, Ms. Stockard. I'm Detective Black. We met in passing a few weeks ago."

She preceded him inside, gesturing that he should follow. "Yes, Detective. I remember. You're homicide, correct?"

"Yes, I am."

"Take a seat. I had to pop out for a minute. My coffeemaker broke yesterday, so I had to sneak some from next door." She placed the mug on one side of her desk and sat behind it. "What can I do for you?"

He explained the reason for his visit.

"Do you remember this case, Detective?"

"Yes."

She studied his face. "Was Mr. Green crazy?"

"In my opinion, he wasn't, but I'm not a doctor."

"Good answer." A grudging smile crossed her lips. "The problem is, as soon as Mr. Green found out the doctor in his case had fudged his credentials, he immediately reported hearing voices."

"Oh, that old song and dance." Hard to keep the sarcasm to himself when they'd seen that tired ploy used so many times.

"I'm afraid so. In order to keep this case moving forward, we'll have to have him re-qualified as sane."

He shrugged. "That shouldn't be a problem. Most offenders don't really know how to fake crazy. They've just watched too much television."

That comment made her chuckle. "I agree. Anyway, it will mean an unavoidable delay, but I'll get a new doctor assigned as soon as possible."

"I appreciate you keeping us informed." He rose. "I won't waste any more of your time."

****

Dayle watched the detective leave, more curious than ever about him now. She'd heard him referred to as the poster boy of the NYPD and expected a vain peacock used to adoration. Instead, he seemed almost shy, certainly introverted. His eyes offered a scientific observation as if he was checking off her personal attributes in his head. His attitude made a refreshing change from the cocky blowhards she ran into all the time.

As he walked down the hall after exiting her office, he didn't appear to notice the surrounding women's eyes tracking his progress. One of the office staff even licked her lips and murmured something to the girl beside her that made them both giggle. She could understand the appeal of his tall, leggy build and thick, dark hair, not to mention those brooding eyes.

His last big case, that of serial killer Cara Belton, had made him infamous. Apparently, he'd long been considered the rising star of his department, but that case had cemented the crown firmly on his head. Still, she definitely got the impression he didn't care about any royal finery or other forms of attention.

She appreciated others who worked hard, as she did, partly out of ambition and partly because they wanted to help create a better world. If money was her motivation, or his, they'd work in the private sector, earning a higher paycheck and better benefits. Checking out the huge stack of files on her desk, she put him out of her mind and got back to work.

Chapter Three

Elijah returned to the office and found Sanchez taking a break. "So, what's she like?" She slumped back in her chair, chewing on a chocolate bar, the second of the day. She'd have to buy her own candy company at this rate.

He shrugged. "She seemed reasonable. She just wants Green assessed by a more reliable doctor."

"I heard she's a looker."

He indulged in the memory of those long, shapely legs and her eyes, the compelling color of good whisky. "Yes, I think most people would consider her quite attractive."

"You know Davis, he knows all the gossip. Looked her up online, like a friggin' stalker. He said she put herself through college modelling for some of the big catalogues."

"It wouldn't surprise me." Glancing at his watch, he grabbed his jacket and keys.

"Where you headed?"

"I have that interview with the third man Bennett dated recently, Jarvis Bentley."

"A lawyer, right?"

"Yes. Personal injury."

"His own firm?"

"Yes."

"Big bucks, then. Where's the office?"

"He's got a suite at the power tower." It was their nickname for the most expensive office building downtown.

"You'll be lucky if they're willing to let one of us in the front door. Have fun."

"Be back in a couple of hours."

"Wanna grab us some lunch from that deli next door? You know the one I mean. They got that great pumpernickel bread."

"Sure." He turned back. "What do you want?"

"Surprise me."

Fifteen minutes later, Elijah parked in the garage underneath the building, guided to an available spot by the attendant after he flashed his badge. A sleek, mirrored elevator whisked him to the twentieth floor with gut-wrenching speed. He located the correct suite easily and found a sleek, young receptionist at a desk, positioned close to the open front doors. Her designer clothes made him feel a little shabby in comparison. The slim blonde stood about five-foot-six and probably wore a size two on a bloated day. "How may I help you?" she asked, giving him a barely veiled once over.

He pulled identification from his pocket. "Detective Black to see Jarvis Bentley."

Lifting her nose a fraction in a time-honored gesture of snobbery, she said, "Do you have an appointment? I'm afraid he's fully booked today." She didn't look remotely sorry about that fact.

"You were told to expect me." He smiled. "I won't take much of his valuable time."

Picking up the phone, she murmured into it. She looked up in response to whatever had been said. "May I ask what this is in reference to?"

"I'm afraid not."

She spoke again, then placed the phone back in its cradle. "He'll be with you in five minutes."

Nodding, he took a seat in one of the plush, cushioned chairs that sat in a semi-circle off to one side. The office décor was modern and white, full of hard angles and lines. The modern look was all the rage, although for the life of him he couldn't understand why. Give him rich color and some quality antiques any day.

As he expected, the promised five minutes turned into ten, then ten into fifteen. Such behavior was a plot used by insecure men to demonstrate a sense of power. Just as he planned on how to circumvent the receptionist, a tall man appeared from behind her. Spouting insincere apologies, he glided forward to meet him. "I'm Jarvis Bentley. So sorry to keep you waiting. Please come with me."

Elijah took note of the man's appearance as he followed him to his office. Bentley's perfect tan looked salon applied, designed to accent his full head of carefully barbered golden hair. His well-cut designer suit probably cost more than Elijah made in a month.

The spacious office had only his massive desk, three chairs, and a teacart. Huge, yawning windows offered an impressive downtown view. Expensive modern art stared at him from the three remaining walls. He wondered if the man could name any of the artists. *Unlikely.* When Bentley turned to gesture him to a padded leather chair, his glacier blue eyes seemed to look right through him. "To what do I owe the honor of a visit from one of the boys in blue?"

The bluff tone didn't fool him. Something about this man raised the hair on the back of his neck. His appearance and the stage setting of the office seemed more like theatrics. It was as if he tried to create the image of perfection without any regard to reality. "I'd like to ask you some questions about Sylvia Bennett."

"I heard about that on the news this morning. What a terrible thing."

If Elijah hadn't studied body language, he might have believed the sincerity of his words. His lips were saying the right things, but the upright frame of his body proved he experienced no particular sadness at all. Grief or even empathy always pulled the shoulders forward. "According to her records, I believe the two of you dated several times in the past two months."

"Yes." He leaned and flicked through some pages on his device. Reading out the three relevant dates, he gave him times for pickup and end times as well. After he provided the information, an odd smile passed his lips.

He took note of the details. "Were these all dinner dates?"

"The first two were." He listed the best restaurants in town, clearly expecting him to be impressed.

Elijah made sure to show no reaction, marking the information in his notebook. "And the third?"

"We went to the opera." Smirking, he added, "I have box seats, of course."

"Had you planned on a fourth date?"

"No."

"May I ask why?"

"There was no physical connection. I didn't see any point in continuing to waste my valuable time when there were many other available women to consider."

He sensed, with some certainty, that this man had

pushed her sexually and been shut down. Was he the man who'd put her off by being too forward? "How would you describe Ms. Bennett in general?"

Leaning back, he steepled his hands. "Attractive, intelligent, a little old-fashioned. She scored about an eight on my preference scale. I prefer a solid ten."

Although he knew the comment was intended to provoke him, he couldn't help responding. "I beg your pardon?"

Bentley laughed, flashing the expensive caps on his gleaming teeth. "Let's be frank, Detective Black. We are both virile men, and the world is jammed full of eager women. Why settle for just another pretty face?"

Seriously, how do men like this ever get a decent date? He ignored the crass comment and moved on. "Did Ms. Bennett ever express concern about anyone following her or making her uncomfortable?"

Again, that odd smile passed his lips. "I'm afraid I can't help you there. Most of our conversations centered on our respective careers, the opera, and art."

"Do you frequently find your dates online?"

"Absolutely. Having dozens of women begging for your company on a nightly basis is an experience well worth savoring. Have you tried it?"

"No."

"You should. You don't know what you're missing."

Elijah was sure this man's initial popularity was only because these women hadn't yet met him. He'd had enough of this braggart. Standing, he shook his hand and left a business card. "If you think of anything that might help—"

"I'll be sure to let you know." As he shut the door,

his last glimpse was a smug smile on the other man's face.

Leaving the building was a relief as if the man's very presence offended the air around him. Elijah waited in line at the delicatessen next door, buying him and Sanchez thick roast beef sandwiches on the famous bread she adored. Deciding to spoil her, he grabbed some chocolate chip cookies, too. He had to struggle to exit with the early lunch crowd clogging the front entrance. Arriving at the car, he lay his food on the passenger seat and closed himself in.

Driving back, he put a deep dive on Bentley on the to-do list. He trusted his instincts—there was something warped about him. It may not have anything to do with Bennett, but he owed it to himself to make sure.

****

The Rhymester spent his days off, and even some of his work hours, stalking his next victim. Oh, she was full of herself, flirting and flaunting with every man to get her way. And it worked. It wasn't just the television cameras that followed her. Men and women alike trailed her to her appearances, desperate to be linked to her rising star.

Pathetic.

Being born beautiful was just genetic fortune, not a personal achievement. The endless search for physical perfection continued with some help from a skilled plastic surgeon. And he knew for a fact that Pamela Clayton had purchased boobs, added a new nose, and wore hair extensions to augment her flowing locks.

Fake everything, including talent.

Women didn't belong on the crime beat. How many talented men had been overlooked during that particular network search? That they'd chosen someone who looked more like a plastic blowup doll was infuriating.

She wasn't the most observant creature, either. He'd been following her, on and off, for weeks—to and from work all over the city, the television station, and at least to the door of her fabulous apartment. Like everyone else, she had a few bad habits. He made note of every one which provided an opportunity.

He carried out his crimes in a way both fast and thorough. Efficient, really, although that sounded more boring than impressive. Thirty seconds was all he required to carry out the deed. Maybe a few bonus moments to watch a victim's last breath trickle from her slender throat. Especially careless walking to and from her car, Clayton frequently leaned into her trunk to fumble with all her odds and ends. That left her no way to see him if he approached her from the rear. That would likely be his best chance.

Oh, to see the look on her face when she realized what vital clue she'd missed. If she didn't recognize him from before, she would as she sucked in her final breath. His first murder had been a cause for gleeful celebration. It had gone perfectly. His confidence level had risen and, now, his hunger for another kill rose.

The insistent clock was ticking in his ear. It wouldn't be long now.

****

Elijah had worked on the case for almost two hours when he realized Sanchez had barely uttered a word. That was a rare enough occasion for him to turn toward her. "Are you okay? You're suspiciously quiet this morning."

She ran a hand through her hair, shoving back the abundant waves. "Jeez, I'm so friggin' distracted."

"What's going on?"

Rapping her knuckles on the desk, she sighed. "Got some personal shit going down."

"Ray okay?"

"He's okay. Not sure I am."

He waited for more information. Sanchez rarely talked about her personal life. She stood and paced around the room, muttering to herself. Finally, she whirled to look at him, her expression one of alarm. "He asked me to marry him last night."

The news surprised him, especially because she didn't look too excited. "That's great! Congratulations." She still didn't smile. "Isn't that a good thing?"

Her voice cracked. "He bought a ring and everything."

Clearly, he didn't understand the point she was trying to make. "That's generally what you do when you want to marry someone. You do love him, right?"

"That's not the point," she huffed, planting her hands on her hips.

"I'd say that's exactly the point. What am I missing?"

"What the hell do I know about that kind of stuff?"

"What, marriage?" Not everyone knew about her lousy childhood, not to mention an ex-boyfriend violent enough to end up serving life in prison. Elijah tried to understand her fears through the perspective of her history. "Strong marriages do exist. You know they do. My parents were very happy together for over fifty years."

"I know." She hung her head and kicked at a gap in

the floor. "We both know that cases like theirs are more of an exception than a rule, though. There's a lot of others that go rollin' down the tracks straight to Crapsville."

"What did you tell him when he asked?"

"I said I'd have to think about it for a while." She sucked in a breath. "He wasn't too happy with me. I mean, not mad, but, you know, disappointed. Like I kicked him in the gut."

A rush of affection for her and her quandary swept over him. "He'll get over it. He's crazy about you, you know."

"Yeah." A ghost of a smile crossed her face. "Maybe he's just crazy to want me."

He walked over and patted her on the back, one of the only forms of affection she usually accepted. As she peered up at him, he said, "Just ask yourself one thing. Whose face do you want to see at the end of a long day?"

"His." She'd responded without pausing.

He took a chance and dropped a kiss on the top of her head. "I think you just answered your own question."

Chapter Four

The next day, he and Sanchez were ordered to do a joint interview with Pamela Clayton. It would focus on how a male/female detective team functioned in the NYPD. It wasn't the best timing, but they weren't given any choice. The commissioner's request took precious time away from their real work, but Elijah understood the value of positive public relations.

At least they liked Clayton, who, despite her fashion doll appearance, was a fair and responsible journalist. They laughed through the interview as they discussed the gritty realities of their job. It only took about an hour of their time, then they all headed out for a much-needed dinner break. Elijah left on foot after seeing them down to the garage in the elevator. Both women were parked on the same level so they continued on together.

He'd walked toward home for just a few minutes when his cellphone rang, the music signaling it was Sanchez. Pausing, he swiped the answer button. "Miss me already?"

"I got stabbed," she gasped. "Hurry."

He hit the emergency number on his cellphone and ran like the track star he'd been in college. "This is Detective Black. Officer down. Precinct garage." He struggled for breath as he lunged for the door, yelling for nearby people to take cover.

He eased inside the door as he heard sirens begin to wail. Under the gloomy light of the garage, there was no one in sight. "Sanchez," he yelled.

"Over here." It wasn't her voice, but Clayton's. "Hurry!" He spied a pale hand waving about halfway down the far side.

"Stay down." He ran to the far end of the cars, using others for cover. Just because a knife had been used didn't mean there were no guns involved. Rounding the last corner, he spied them. His partner lay crumpled on the pavement, Clayton cradling her head and shoulders on her lap. As he crouched beside them, he heard the shouts of others coming to help. "How bad?"

Blood ran down her arm as she tried to point to the injury. "Just above the vest," she whispered.

He tried not to worry that it was on the side of her heart, close to her armpit. Easing her arms out of the vest, he looked. Blood drenched the entire side of her blouse. He applied pressure to the wound, and she winced, cursing him under her breath.

"Let me take a look." A male emergency medical technician materialized out of nowhere and pushed him to the side. He ripped her shirt open for a better view of the wound. "Just the one strike?"

"Ain't that enough?" she muttered, sucking in a breath.

"You just keep being a smartass, Sanchez, and you'll be fine." Reaching into his case, he pulled out some large cotton squares and packed them around the wound, securing them with tape. He gestured to his partner who stood next to a gurney, behind the others. "We're going to take you to the hospital now. You hangin' in?"

"Hangin' in," she repeated, dredging up a weak smile. She peered up at Elijah, tears brimming in the corners of her eyes. "Call Ray. Tell him I'm sorry."

"Tell him yourself." He squeezed her hand. "I'll be right behind you."

He watched, feeling helpless, as they loaded her into the back of the ambulance, slamming the doors. The driver jumped in and gunned the engine. As the vehicle swerved onto the street, siren wailing, he turned to Clayton. "Tell me what happened."

Her eyes looked glazed. He took off his jacket to place it around her shoulders. Without it, she could go into shock. "He came up behind me. I caught sight of him in the reflection of my car, his hand raised as he ran toward me, holding a knife. I screamed, turned around, and hit him with my briefcase." She started to cry but continued to speak through gasps of air. "Sanchez came out of nowhere, like a ninja. She jumped on his back, and they fought. I didn't know how to help her."

"Did she have a weapon?"

"I think she reached for her knife, but he knocked it out of her hand."

He paused to tell one of the others to look for it, then turned back to Clayton. "Which direction did he run toward?"

She pointed to the far corner exit, guilt creating lines on her face. "If I wasn't in the way, she could have used her gun."

"It's not your fault. It's a miracle he didn't get you. What did he look like?"

"Tall, stocky. He had a black knit thing over his

face. I could only see his eyes, nose and mouth."

"Is there anything else that you noticed?"

"N-no. I don't think so. It all happened so quickly."

By this time, the place was swarming with cops of every description. Leaving the reporter with a beat cop, he glanced around. He located his lieutenant, conveying the description, and arranged to have Jones and Hadley take over the scene so he could follow Sanchez to the hospital. Both detectives had already arrived, winded from running. They could head up the search for the assailant and, according to the curses he heard, were already frustrated they'd missed him by mere minutes. Before Elijah left the parking lot, he called Ray at the hotel and told him where he could go to be with Sanchez.

He hadn't suffered real fear in a while, but his pulse beat a tattoo in his chest. She was family. Not just NYPD family, but the only family he had. If anything happened to her, he would never forgive himself.

Why hadn't he accompanied them to their cars as his manners dictated? Sanchez would have teased him unmercifully, but it would have prevented this mayhem. The painful reason he hadn't was that he knew Clayton had an interest in him, but he thought of her only as a casual friend. It made his usual polite habits a little awkward because he didn't want any misunderstandings between them.

Arriving at the hospital, he parked the car in the crowded emergency lot, his police tag in clear sight. He hurried through the automatic glass sliding doors. The busy female clerk at the front desk told him to sit tight, she would find out where Sanchez had been taken and her condition. Unable to sit, he paced back and forth.

After a few moments, an older, bespectacled doctor came out to speak to him, pulling him to a quiet corner. "They are preparing your partner for the operating room. She has one deep stab wound in the vicinity of her heart. At this point, we think it missed everything vital, but we can't guarantee that until we get into surgery and have a look."

"How serious is her blood loss?"

"A bit of good news there at least. She's getting a transfusion, but it's more of a safeguard at this point." He smiled. "She's quite a character and a fighter. Don't worry, we'll take excellent care of her. She mentioned a boyfriend?"

"I called him. He's on his way."

"Good. I'll be back as soon as we're out of surgery."

"Thank you, Doctor."

The spacious waiting room began to fill up with cops, their lieutenant among them. Some with the same blood type as Sanchez donated to the blood bank while they waited. After a while, Clayton showed up with her crew and parked quietly in one corner. Other people waiting stared at the crowd with curiosity as discussion caused the noise level to rise. A short while later, Ray shoved through the crowd, searching for him. He stood, lifting a hand to catch his attention.

His frantic friend dodged through the crowd on his way over, his face pale. "How bad is it?"

"It's serious, but she seems to be holding her own." He told him what had happened and what the doctor said.

"Is it this same asshole you're looking for?"

"We don't know for sure. A team is searching for

the assailant right now. We'll look into that possibility."

"She just had to be the friggin' hero." Distraught, he put his face in his hands.

Elijah patted his arm in an attempt to console him. "It's who she is. But she's tough, and she stayed conscious the entire time. Fighters always make the best recoveries in situations like this."

"I asked her to marry me." He spoke the words like an admission of guilt as if that had caused her bad luck.

"Yes, she told me." Elijah tried to find the words to reassure him. "She loves you very much, you know. She's just scared. With her background, she questions everything about family life. She never had anyone around to show her just how good it can be."

"Honest to God, I would never hurt her. Swear on a stack of Bibles." Making the figure of a cross, he raised his head and struggled to smile. "She's the spicy meatball to my spaghetti."

He thought about Ray's big Italian family and realized he couldn't have put it any better. "It's going to work out fine. You'll see." He willed his prayers into fact.

"There's one thing I don't understand. Why didn't she just shoot him?"

"He attacked the other woman first. She couldn't get a safe angle with her in the way."

The expected two-hour operation took almost three. When the doctor finally came through the doors, the whole crowd of her friends rushed him in the bid for information. He put out his hands to slow them down and raised his voice to be heard above the racket of the crowd. "Who's Ray?"

He stepped forward as they cleared the way for

them to connect. "That's me."

The doctor nodded, his fatigue evident in the dark shadows under his eyes. "She's in recovery, doing well. She asked for you as soon as she opened her eyes. The wound is deep, but it missed her heart. Barring complications, she's going to be fine."

He brushed away tears of relief with the back of one hand. "Thanks, Doc. How soon can I see her?"

"As soon as we move her out of the intensive care unit to a regular bed, I'll send someone to come and get you. To be honest, I planned to leave her there overnight, but since the injury didn't affect any major organs, she can move on and free up the bed. We've got an overflow crowd tonight."

The encouraging news worked its way through the crowd, and eventually most of the cops went back to work or home to get some much-needed rest. His lieutenant called him away for a quiet word. "The security cameras caught a few frames of the assailant, but he got away. Dressed all in black with a mask covering his face, so that's not much help. Clayton said something interesting when we interviewed her, though."

"What's that?"

"She said when the attacker cursed at Sanchez, his voice seemed familiar, but she couldn't place it. We have no way of knowing if that's just her imagination, but she's quite observant."

"Pretty reckless of him to try and grab her right here in our precinct building. What the hell was he thinking?"

"Stupid, really, but he did manage to escape. If it's the same guy, I think getting away with the first murder so far made him over-confident." He sighed. "I'm heading home. It's been a long day. You staying?"

"For now."

"Let me know if anything changes. I'll have my assistant send some flowers from all of us."

"With all due respect, sir, she might appreciate a snack basket more."

A glimmer of a smile crossed his face. "Good point. Thanks."

"Yes, sir."

A short while later, a nurse came and took Ray to Sanchez's room. Thirty minutes after that, he came back out, smiling. "They're gonna let me stay overnight on a cot next to her. She wants to see you for a minute." They walked down the hall together. "She said yes."

"Good for you. I knew she'd come around. Congratulations."

Ray waited in the hall outside to give them some privacy. Elijah entered the room and moved to sit beside the bed. She looked so defenseless, her cheek resting against the white sheets of the bed, her hair a messy tumble. Her exhausted eyes inched open, struggling to focus. "Hey."

"Hey, yourself." Reaching down, he squeezed her hand. "I hear you took the plunge. Congratulations."

"Yeah." She sucked in a breath, wincing. "I told God if he just let me live through this, I was gonna stop bein' such a dope and marry that man."

Her words made him chuckle. "So, where's that fancy ring you were talking about?"

"He's got it on a chain around his neck, next to his cross." She rolled her eyes. "He was gonna put it on me, and I told him he was nuts. I'll get mugged while

I'm sleeping for sure. That'd be my luck."

"Good idea. Just make sure to put it on as soon as you get home."

"Yeah." She squinted up at him, then raised a hand to shield against the glaring light. "The guys didn't catch him, did they?"

He shook his head. "Clayton said she thought his voice sounded familiar, though."

"He didn't talk much, other than some bullshit." She smiled. "I was too busy kickin' him in the nuts to hear it anyway."

"Good for you."

"The bastard called me a spic whore." Shrugging, she continued, "I been called worse."

"Well, Clayton compared you to a ninja. That's more your style. She's signing up to be your new best friend."

"Yeah, 'cause we got so much in common." She went through the details of the attack again, but he could tell she'd pushed herself far enough.

When Ray rejoined them, Elijah left and went home so she could get some rest. The sight of them, their hands clasped together, gave him hope for the future.

He would figure out who attacked Clayton and Sanchez if it took his last breath.

Chapter Five

Ready to take a break from legal maneuvering, assistant district attorney Stockard was planning to call Detective Black when she glanced up and saw him standing in her doorway. "Oh, Detective Black. I was just going to call you."

"Call me Elijah."

"Okay. I'm Dayle." A flush of attraction traveled through her, and she ignored it. "I wanted you to know Mr. Green was re-examined yesterday. Much to his chagrin, he was once again judged mentally competent to stand trial. We will proceed with all haste."

"I'm pleased to hear that. Thanks for getting the case back on track."

She wished her persistent headache would ease off so she could enjoy this man's company for a few moments. It was a nice way to break up her grueling day. "I hear your partner will be released from the hospital tomorrow. I'm relieved to hear it."

"Thank you. That's actually why I dropped by. Sanchez and her fiancé, Ray, are having an engagement party at her place on Saturday night. I was wondering if you would be interested in going with me."

"Wow, she sure bounces back quickly. I'm surprised they don't wait a while. A six-day recovery isn't much."

"I thought so, too, but apparently they're impatient

to celebrate both the engagement and her recovery. If I know Ray, he'll take care of everything and won't let her move a muscle."

"Well, in that case..." She met his calm gaze. Those serious eyes lightened with the hint of a smile. "I would enjoy going with you. What can I bring?"

"I'm taking wine. Perhaps an easy dessert?"

"Done." She wrote her address on a notepad, tore the page off, and handed it to him.

"I'll pick you up at seven, if that's okay."

"Perfect. Is it casual dress?"

He hadn't asked, but couldn't see his partner putting on a fashion show. "Yes."

"Great. I'll see you then." He disappeared down the hall as silently as he'd come. He was uncommonly graceful for a big man. She wondered if he could dance. She enjoyed dancing.

She hadn't dated anyone in a long time. Elijah was the first man who had appealed to her since her move to New York. If she was honest with herself, she had to admit her dating drought had lasted a lot longer than that. As a celebration, she might even treat herself to a new casual skirt. Lately, her wardrobe screamed of long, dedicated office hours and not much else. One woman could only wear so many suits. Maybe it was time to search out a few, more feminine offerings.

Her meagre social life was an ongoing challenge. An ever-growing case load demanded long hours and, frankly, finding a significant other had taken a back seat for way too long. She didn't really believe in the myth of happily ever after anymore, but a warm body to sleep next to held some appeal. Her oldest friend, Cynthia, had told her that her 'picker' was broken when it came to choosing men. If her disastrous first marriage hadn't been proof enough of that theory, she wasn't sure what would. Almost a decade had passed, and the haunting memories still served as a reminder to use an abundance of caution.

She'd heard the gossip about Elijah. According to the women staff members, he was exceedingly picky and very private. A few of them joked about trying to toss their hat in his ring only to have him politely hand it back. Since she was rather choosy herself, she couldn't hold that tendency against him. It made, instead, a point in his favor. She found far too many men aggressive in their pursuit of a woman. For her, that became the biggest turnoff of them all.

Now, she had something fun to look forward to on the weekend. In the meantime, she got back to work.

****

The little bitch had survived. *Damn her.*

He hadn't just missed his target, but now he had to worry about whether he'd given himself away. Long after he'd fled the scene, he remembered cursing as he fought. Clayton had reacted more aggressively than he'd anticipated, and her fighting back threw him off his game. To have Sanchez leap on his back like a damn monkey immediately after unbalanced him and almost stopped him in his tracks. At least he'd managed to injure her, get away clean, and circle back within minutes.

The lucky knife strike an inch above her vest ended up being his one stroke of good fortune. He'd been flailing, desperate to reach vulnerable flesh. It should have punctured her heart and killed her. He wished it had and would have been thrilled to see the blood drain from her as he escaped. Now, he had to totally rethink his strategy and select a new target. Both Clayton and Sanchez would be on their guard for the foreseeable future.

But he had a bounty of deserving bitches from which to choose. It seemed as if everywhere he looked, females were taking over, emasculating men with their aggressive agenda.

Choosing someone new might offer him a fun opportunity to enlarge his plans.

****

In his home office early Saturday morning, Elijah studied the proposals printed out and stacked on his desk. Despite his best efforts to contain any gossip, word had leaked that he'd inherited money and would be administering some of it to worthy causes in the near future. Since then, he received daily demands for money from any number of sources, some worthy and many others not. Luckily, he'd had the foresight to direct the deluge through a nearby post office box. He picked the mail up most days on the way home from work, scooping the contents into a plastic bag to carry home with him.

It would get worse if they ever figured out he would be giving all of the money away, not just the half as his benefactor had suggested. Not many men inherited money from a serial killer. He pushed thoughts of Cara away.

He had culled all of the latest requests down to the half dozen he thought really had merit. As Cara had intended, they all provided some level of assistance to abused women and children. Some offered secure housing, food, or protection, and one place provided all three. Others involved free legal assistance or job training. The last offered gave psychological assistance to deal with the unavoidable emotional trauma.

After choosing them, he had asked for an in-depth financial report on each one. The money he awarded had to be carefully managed and spent. It was essential to make it stretch as far as possible, so they could help as many people as the funds could reach. Four reports had already come in. He glanced through the endless lines of columns, searching for any red flags that might indicate sloppy management.

As soon as he'd read them all and been satisfied, he would ask for a personal tour of each facility. If they all passed his inspection, he would then have to decide how much to give them. They had included a 'wish list' at his request. He would want to ascertain that their priorities were well thought out.

Working his way through these projects had helped pull him out of the funk Cara's tragic death had triggered. One of the downfalls of his job was that sometimes it seemed like the bad guys were winning. Criminals avoided prosecution on technicalities all the time. If he could guarantee that steps were being taken to help others who'd suffered abuse as she had, it would help him feel whole again.

Sanchez had been the one to boot his ass until he agreed to return to the routine of his regular life. He would never forget that, even though she didn't understand his feelings about Cara, she had supported him. He could never understand why, before they had paired up, she'd gone through three previous partners. When he'd been assigned to work with her, he'd been teased and told good luck.

The truth was, he couldn't imagine a better partner for him. Her mind worked in a totally different way than his, and that proved to be helpful. It offered him a different perspective. As hard as he might try, he could never understand what it was to be a woman in a traditionally male occupation. Especially not a Hispanic woman. Her viewpoint, formed by a far different background, helped him deal more effectively with victims.

And, thank goodness, she had an aptitude with any sort of technology, something he lacked. They had an agreement which suited them both. She dealt with those challenges, and he dealt with the brass. She was smart enough to realize that demonstrating tact to her superiors presented a challenge for her. For her, a spade was a spade, not a gently curved shovel.

Glancing at his watch, he realized the time had come to head back to the office. Homicide detectives in the middle of a major case didn't have the luxury of a weekend off. A few hours was the best he could hope for at those times. Spending the afternoon poring over the information didn't result in any more leads, though, so he gave up at eight p.m. and headed home.

The next day, Sanchez was released from hospital. She kept encouraging the nurse's aide who transported her to the exit to pop some wheelies, but he refused, rolling his eyes. Elijah and Ray went together to see her safely home, then her fiancé rushed back to work, repeating cautions as he closed the door behind himself.

"Can you keep me company for a few minutes?" Ray had told her to stay on the couch and wrap herself in an old quilt that lay folded there which she grudgingly did.

"Of course." He settled in the armchair next to her. The fact that she'd obeyed any orders showed him she didn't feel the best.

"They're keeping me on bedrest for at least a week. Maybe more." Her incredulous tone made him smile.

"A knife wound is nothing to take lightly."

"Not a big deal. It missed all the important stuff."

"Just barely. And a knife wound is always a big deal." He mentally searched for something to cheer her up. "You have the engagement party coming up on Saturday to look forward to."

"That's true." A smile lightened her expression. "I told Ray he doesn't have to cook because it's pot luck, but he will anyway. We'll have enough food to start our own grocery store."

"Are you sure you shouldn't wait until you're a little stronger? You can't afford to overdo it."

She shook her head. "Nah, Ray's real excited, and he said he'd do all the work. I'll just sit here like a lump and let myself get waited on." Shifting made her wince. "You gonna bring a date?"

"Believe it or not, I am."

"What did you say?" She tilted her head so her one ear faced him. "I must be hearin' things."

Her antics made him laugh. "Your hearing's just fine."

"Well, spill the goods. Who is it?"

"I asked Dayle Stockard. She's nice, and she doesn't know many people here yet."

Surprise raised her eyebrows. "Jeez, good for you. Trying to beat everyone to the starting gate?"

"Yes. I'm pretty sure she could pick and choose from any number of men."

"She must be smarter than average if she picked you. What's she like?"

"That's what I plan to find out. I know she's attractive and intelligent. That's a good place to start."

"I'll cross my fingers that you don't screw it up," she teased.

"Appreciate it. I need all the help I can get."

"Did ya see the article Clayton wrote about the two of us?"

It had taken up half of the front page. "I did. You make pretty impressive frontpage copy. Heroine of the day."

"She made it sound like a bigger deal than it was."

"Don't sell yourself short. It is a big deal. You saved her life."

Snorting a laugh, she said, "I guess that's my fifteen minutes of fame. Just had to suffer a knife wound to get it."

"I guess so."

After fidgeting, she finally settled in. "Listen, I know I'm not supposed to work, but can you at least give me some computer stuff I can do from here?"

"Of course." He knew her well enough to know she'd get stir crazy and do too much if he didn't agree. "Can you do a deep dive on the three men Sylvia dated? Two of them looked totally legit to me. The third raised my hackles."

"What the hell are hackles, anyway?"

"The upright hairs on a dog's back."

She shook her head. "You know some strange crap."

"You don't know the half of it."

"So, let's see, number three was Bentley

somebody, right?"

"Jarvis Bentley. The lawyer, remember?"

"Got it." She leaned over to scrawl the name on a pad left on the coffee table.

"And maybe you could call Pamela Clayton and chat about her recent dating life. Ask her if she's had problems with anyone lately."

She nodded, scrawling a note. Looking up, she grinned. "You afraid she might try and nibble on your tootsies if you ask her?"

An unfortunate flush heating his cheeks would egg her on. "It's just a little awkward, that's all. She's a good person, but I don't want her to think I'm asking for myself."

"She's too flashy for you. I mean, I like her, but I catch your drift." She batted her eyes. "You could just roll around the sheets, have a good workout, and call it a day."

"I know I'm boring, but that's not really my style."

"Mine, either, anymore. Guess we're both getting old."

"That's true." Glancing at his watch, he stood. "I'd better get going. Can I get you anything before I leave?"

"Just the remote and my laptop. I already got my phone." She glanced around. "Maybe my gun, too. If that sonofabitch comes back for another try, I can blast him back out the way he came."

Fetching the items from the other side of the room, he settled them beside her and kissed her on the head. "Call me if you dig up anything of interest. And get a lot of rest, okay?"

"Will do, I promise."

Back at his desk thirty minutes later, he spent some time comparing Bennett's murder with the attack on Sanchez and Pamela Clayton. One used a gun, one a knife. One took place at night, one during the day. Did the same perp do both? *Impossible to say.* On paper, you'd think it would have to be two different assailants, but his gut warned him of a different story. In this business, there was little room for coincidence.

Both his partner and the dedicated newswoman worked on multiple criminal cases at the same time. Their attacker could be anyone from past or current cases. That opened up a huge, overwhelming number of suspects. Or is that the kind of thing their attacker wanted them to waste time on?

Damn it. He couldn't risk a repeat performance. Sanchez might not survive a second time. And she would always rush to the rescue—one of the things he admired most about her.

The only clue they had culled from the crime was that Clayton thought she'd recognized her attacker's voice. Could she be correct, or was that just a case of her grasping at straws in an effort to help? In his experience, you would only remember someone's voice if you heard it multiple times. Did that mean it might be someone she knew? He texted his partner a message to include asking Clayton about the voice again. Maybe she had remembered something else that might help.

Chapter Six

By the time Elijah left the office at the end of the day, Sanchez had got back to him about a few things. Apparently, Clayton had remembered nothing more about the voice which was driving her to distraction. The first two men on Bennett's list still looked clean, other than a few harmless parking tickets. She found the same during an initial look at Bentley, but promised to look deeper the following day.

He went to bed early to catch up on his sleep and was glad he had when the phone rang at two a.m. A dead woman had been discovered in her parked car outside an upscale nightclub in the east end. He'd been contacted once the first officer on scene had found the body with three bullet wounds identical to Sylvia Bennett's. Wishing for a break rarely worked. He sat on the side of the bed for a minute, trying to summon some energy.

Once in the car, it took him another frustrating twenty minutes to make it to the club. Even in the middle of the night, when most of the public were snug in their beds, the crime had attracted a lot of attention. Civilians and multiple news crews cluttered up the approach to the crime scene. Parking as close as he could, he climbed out of his car and headed over, ignoring the shouted questions as gathered reporters recognized him. He crossed the asphalt parking lot and ducked under the yellow crime scene tape.

A local patrolman he recognized hurried up to him. Tall and stocky, Seth Parker nodded a greeting, his uniform stretching over broad shoulders. A hard-working cop who'd been on the streets for a few years, he knew his stuff. "Seth," he said, shaking his hand. "What have we got?"

"An anonymous caller phoned and told dispatch a lady in this parking lot needed assistance. We checked her pulse to be sure, but she's been dead a while. When we saw her wounds, we called it in and waited for you. Crime scene is three minutes out, medical examiner right behind them."

"Great. Thanks."

"How's Sanchez?"

"Not too happy to be left out of the action, but she's doing well." He walked and took a closer look at the scene, the other man at his side. He saw the blonde hair first, cascading down to end at the top of her breasts. As he moved closer, he saw she wore the quintessential little black dress with blood saturating the front. The glare from the light above allowed him to differentiate between black material and the blotch of dark red. He could barely see the details of her pale face because she had slumped forward from the impact of the bullets. "Anyone see anything?"

"Not that we've found thus far. It was getting close to closing when we arrived, and most people had already left."

He turned to scan the crowd. "Were you able to catch any other patrons before they left?"

"There were only two customers left by the time I sent a man in. Both women. They're waiting for permission to go home. Said they didn't even notice her."

"Check their identification, verify their personal information and let them go home. I'll contact them tomorrow. Have the staff wait." He knew they'd grumble and complain, but they might have noticed something important.

"Will do."

The crime scene van showed up, disgorging three technicians who got right down to work. They were closely followed by the medical examiner who climbed out, an annoyed frown creasing his face. Who could blame him? Come dawn, he still had a full work day and a dozen corpses lying in wait for his arrival. He needed a new assistant.

Elijah stood back and allowed them to do their jobs. Before the doctor released the body, he had a final look. "She's only been dead about an hour, Elijah," Dr. Hayes said. "He's getting cocky." Her leather purse lay on the seat beside her where the technician had left it. After confirming they had dusted it, Elijah put on gloves and opened it. A slender wallet, a few makeup tubes and a cellphone waited there.

Inside her slim wallet, he found a few credit cards and her driver's license. Her name was Alia Marks, thirty-eight years old. A quick online check proved his suspicion; another well-known professional woman. She was a successful fashion designer at the top of her game.

Not anymore.

He waited as the medical examiner released the body. The attendants loaded it on the gurney and trundled it away. A number of onlookers taking cellphone pictures of the poor woman's body depressed him. When did people turn into vultures fighting over a corpse? It demonstrated an astounding lack of empathy that seemed like the norm these days.

He watched as her immaculate luxury car was loaded onto a truck bed, then, ignoring shouted questions from the press, made his way into the nightclub. The interior was almost glaring, but it might have been his tired eyes. Elegant black and white décor was everywhere, the stark colors broken only by vases of pale pink roses.

Seth waved him over to an imposing man who wore an expensive designer suit along with a pronounced frown. His slicked back hair and manicured nails equaled a professional appearance that made him the likely manager. "Black, this is Roger Corrigan. He's the manager of this club. Mr. Corrigan, Detective Black is in charge of this investigation."

The man gave him a once over, swiping a practiced hand over his platinum hair. "Detective Black." He shook his hand. "I'm not sure how we can help you. Apparently, no one in here saw anything."

"Did you know Ms. Marks personally?"

"Not well, but I recognize her. She's a regular."

"And she was alone tonight? She didn't arrive with anyone?"

"That's correct. She had drinks with a few of our other regulars, then left. That appears to be her normal routine."

He scanned around for cameras, not seeing any. "Do you have any security measures?"

"No cameras inside. Our patrons expect us to provide the highest level of privacy."

"How about outside?"

"Yes, we have a camera on each corner of the building and one by the entrance."

As he wondered how to best deal with them, Seth stepped up. "If you like, I can take care of them for you. I'm a bit of an E-geek."

At least he wouldn't have to worry about fumbling along without his partner. "That would be great. Let me know if you find anything worth pursuing."

While Seth took charge of the electronics, Elijah spoke to each of the eleven staff members left waiting in the staff lounge, but none had anything interesting to contribute. With help from Seth's partner and a few others, he processed everyone and let them go home. The usual grumbles followed them out. When he turned a few minutes later, Seth was waiting, a DVD in his outstretched hand. "I got a copy for you to check out, but all you can see is a figure dressed in black, head to toe. The entire attack took about thirty seconds before he made his escape."

"Thanks. We'll let the technicians take a look at it. Maybe they can enhance it and see something that might help."

At just after seven a.m., they wrapped up the scene and he and Seth headed to a nearby breakfast joint for some food. He treated, because he was happy Seth had been around to help keep things together. They relaxed in a back booth and ignored the other diners. "Thanks for logging in the overtime on this. I appreciate the help."

Seth rested his forearms on the table. "You're welcome. You got much on this guy yet? He seems to have a major grudge against the ladies."

"Still in the early stages, but, no, not much yet."

"We can at least estimate his height from tonight's footage."

He was impressed Seth had caught that. "You're right. That's something at least."

They ordered eggs, bacon, and toast, avoiding the temptation of more fattening options. A waitress left them with a jug of coffee to save herself extra trips. The piping hot food appeared within ten minutes, and they dug in. Pausing between mouthfuls, Seth said, "I heard your partner got engaged. What, did getting shot rattle her?"

"I think she just realized she was wasting precious time. Ray's a good man for her."

"Big Italian guy, right? Wasn't he on the force for a while?"

"Yes. He has a job as head of hotel security now."

Seth poured them each more coffee. "Did I hear you paid a visit to Jarvis Bentley the other day?"

The question caught him by surprise. "Is that what you heard?" He met the other man's gaze, curious about the reason for his question.

"Hey, you don't have to tell me anything about your case. I know it's high profile." He met his gaze. "The thing is, I have a friend who mentioned she saw you going into his office. I was thinking about calling you, but things have been hectic. I didn't want to butt in when it might not mean anything."

"Do you know something about Jarvis Bentley I should be aware of?"

He shrugged. "My sister manages a nice restaurant downtown, and she had a run in with him. I had to have a little talk to him, man to man, to straighten him out."

Interesting. "Can I assume this was a no-fists conversation?"

He grinned. "You can. It was tempting, though. He's a slimy sonofabitch, despite all the fancy clothes."

"What exactly did he do?"

"He was at the restaurant for a lunch meeting with some other men. After they left, he asked her out for dinner. She said no, thanks, she was involved with someone." Anger made his jaw tighten.

"Did he push his luck?"

He nodded. "When she left to go home that night, he followed her to her place. She told him to get lost, and he shoved her up against the car. Held her so tight, she had bruises around her arms."

"Did she call 911?"

"Nah, she kneed him in the gonads." A smile glimmered, lightening his expression. "My sister's nobody's fool. Anyway, she told me, and I felt the need to intervene. I just had a pointed conversation with him and told him to back off."

"That's more restraint than most brothers would have shown under the circumstances."

"Thanks. If he hadn't stopped, I might have reported him whether she liked it or not." He shrugged. "Anyway, you can see why I wasn't sure I should say something. Women deal with this shit every day, but, if you're looking into him, I thought I should give you a heads up."

"I appreciate it, Seth. I'll get Sanchez to delve a little deeper."

Driving back to the precinct, he thought about what Seth had told him. Was Bentley a strong suspect or just another sex-starved moron?

He arrived back at his desk and took a moment to text his partner this new information. Right after that, he received a text telling him the autopsy would take place at two p.m. They had been pushed almost to the front of the line because of the likelihood of another connected murder soon.

Tracking down leads took most of the afternoon. As before, the results from the autopsy were depressing. These scenes were so clean, as if they'd been sanitized. Other than determining the killer's approximate height, five-nine to five-ten, from the security footage, there was nothing more to be found.

****

Saturday night, Elijah didn't have as much time to get ready for his date as he wanted. He had spent most of the day either working or studying the material on his six possible donation options. While he had a few minutes, he set up a visit to the first facility.

After grabbing a quick shower, he climbed into the freshly ironed khakis and blue polo shirt he'd chosen the previous night. He'd forgotten to buy a gift bag for the wine, but he didn't think Sanchez would care. With one last check in the hallway mirror, he left the house.

Arriving at Dayle's stylish apartment complex a few minutes early, he was surprised to find her already waiting in the lobby. Pleasure flickered through him at the sight of her as the doorman opened the door and she came outside. She wore a simple turquoise cotton skirt that brushed her ankles paired with a white silk blouse. Silver earrings hung from her earlobes. Her long, dark hair hung down around her shoulders, tamed by a simple band.

He exited the car and strode up to her. "Hi. You

could have waited upstairs."

"I'm always early." She smiled. "It's a curse or a gift, depending on your perspective. I thought I may as well save you the trouble of coming up."

Taking the plastic covered plate of cookies she carried, he placed it on the floorboards in back. He opened the passenger door for her, surprised at the case of unfamiliar nerves dancing up his back. On the short drive to his partner's place, they talked mostly about the engaged couple and how Sanchez was feeling.

"Ours isn't a gentle world, is it?" she said.

"I'm afraid not."

By the time they arrived, they could hear laughter guiding the way down the hall. The party had already started. Inside the open door, they found Sanchez perched on the sofa, like a queen surrounded by her subjects. She looked less pale and better rested, the shadows gone from under her eyes. Dressed head-to-toe in bright orange, she kept everyone's attention from her nest. He worked his way to her, pulling Dayle along by the hand. He introduced them and saw Sanchez eye her. "Nice to meet ya. Like your skirt."

"Oh, thanks. I wanted something comfy and fun." She stopped to admire his partner's ring which sparkled under the lights. The single diamond was surrounded by a swirl of gold. "It's beautiful."

"Thanks. He did a good job pickin' it out."

He glanced around. "Where's Ray?"

"In the kitchen. You can leave the wine and dessert there. He'll take care of it."

Some other women showed up to inspect her ring, so they moved to the kitchen. Ray kissed Dayle on each cheek with an enthusiastic smack, startling her. "Look at this beauty!" he said, holding both her hands. He looked at Elijah. "Man, your taste is improving."

"It certainly is," he replied, handing him the cookies and wine to add to the other plates and bottles on the crowded counter. Ray gave Dayle the third degree until another arriving couple distracted him.

The party proved to be everything he expected: loud and fun. Surprised to see how easily Dayle fit in, he stayed at her side as they worked her way around the crowded room. Knowing he had a tendency to sit and study rather than participate, he tried his best to take part for her sake. It ended up to be quite relaxing. They drank lightly, sampling several dishes and desserts throughout the evening.

They left around midnight when the booze-inspired singing started. If the neighbors weren't in attendance, the noise level might have been a problem. He realized Dayle was humming one of the songs blaring out as they rode the elevator down. "I hope I didn't drag you out of there too early," he said. "My ears were starting to ring."

"Oh, no, it was perfect. They really are a fun group of people."

"I'm glad you enjoyed yourself."

"I especially liked your partner and Ray. She seems like such a firecracker, but her eyes are so expressive. And Ray, he just likes everyone, doesn't he?"

"Yes. They're good people. It was nice not to have work interrupt for a change. I guess miracles happen now and then."

Reaching ground level, they strolled outside and down the street. They transitioned from bright light to dim on the way to his car. Elijah's eyes scanned their surroundings from habit. He noticed she did the same thing, and he mentioned it as they climbed into the car. "You can never be too careful," she replied. "I guess our jobs teach us that every day."

They discussed the constant demands of their careers on the short drive home. Although she said he could drop her off at the entrance, he insisted on seeing her to her door. She greeted the doorman with a smile as they moved past him to the elevator. The trip to the seventh floor was quick. After she opened the door to her apartment, he leaned to kiss her cheek. "I hope we can do this again soon."

Her gaze met his. "I'd like that very much."

He watched as she closed the door, waited until he heard the lock slide shut. That had been the most relaxed date he'd had in years. And, better yet, she'd said she'd be willing to do it again. Simple chemistry had been there in the way she smiled at him.

He mused about it on the drive home. His heavy workload might be easier to handle if he actually had some kind of social life outside the job. And her hours were as exhausting as his, so she shouldn't find the constant interruptions out of the ordinary.

Smiling, he realized Sanchez would call him in the morning, asking how the date went.

For a change, he would have positive news to tell her.

Chapter Seven

Glancing around her apartment at the few boxes still not unpacked made Dayle sigh. Her loose, cotton nightie billowed around her as she went to the refrigerator for a glass of water.

Elijah seemed almost too good to be true, she thought, as she prepared for bed. He was attractive, funny, and had great manners, something sadly missing in a lot of men. The affection and concern he'd shown his feisty partner had been nice to watch. At the party, he'd let everyone else do most of the talking, but had stayed engaged. His dark eyes drank in every detail of his surroundings. She liked his quiet confidence.

Most people thought cops made terrible lovers, especially homicide cops. They worked horrendous hours, and their private lives got interrupted by emergency calls all the time. She wondered, though, whether someone like Elijah might suit her well. Men often referred to her as 'too independent,' but that's what would be required when your significant other might be frequently on the job at strange hours. And, God knows, her work hours had never been nine to five.

She never kissed on the first date and had been called hopelessly backward because of it. Elijah's gentle kiss on the cheek had been just the right touch— a simple gesture to convey interest.

Her first marriage had been to a so-called alpha

male. She had significant scars, both physical and emotional, to show for it. No, this tall, leggy detective with the intuitive gaze suited her well so far. It would be interesting to investigate the possibilities.

Tomorrow, she might even get around to unpacking those last few boxes.

****

On Monday morning, Elijah sat at his desk, paging through Alia Marks' black, leather-bound diary. They had discovered it in the packed drawer of her nightstand along with a rather daunting selection of brightly colored sex toys. Everything from dildos to ticklers and handcuffs jammed the space. Inside the journal, he found detailed stories about family life and work along with a rather unusual set of charts. Although he'd heard of men rating women they dated, he'd never heard of a woman doing such a crass thing. And yet, here it was, not only a five-star system, but an actual graph showing each partner's sexual performance. She used some rather clever analogies to describe men's private parts. Sanchez would have howled with laughter, but he skipped over most of it. It actually embarrassed him, and he thought he'd seen it all by now.

Apparently, Alia had a rather robust sex drive. It appeared that she met most of the men on the same website their first victim had used. He made a note to have Sanchez check into that company further.

A lot of the men's names listed were white collar professionals, their jobs listed on the chart. No plumbers or garbagemen for her. He couldn't imagine her dates' scores from her rather harsh judging system would please them. If this was the only diary, she had been doing this for almost two years now. The more recent liaisons interested him, though, and he paged through to a place six weeks in the past. It wasn't long before a name he recognized jumped out at him.

Jarvis Bentley. That guy just kept popping up like a bad smell.

Well, he certainly got around, didn't he? She'd had three dates with him he could easily find. His scores were mediocre, two to three stars, which didn't surprise him. She had written a long diatribe in the final note underneath.

Loser!!! After the first two dates, he said it was time to split the dinner bill!

When I protested, he said, "You're not that great in the sack, hon."

I told him if he could last for more than three minutes, it might help.

He wasn't smirking too much when I poured a very expensive glass of wine on his lap.

I guess he paid the dinner bill after all because I left.

The next day, he left a message on my cell, calling me a worthless whore.

Worthless? Never!!!

He shook his head. All that drama would make his head ache, but some people appeared to be addicted to such histrionics. His phone rang, the music startling in the quiet room. It was Sanchez. "Hey. I thought you'd sleep in until noon."

"Nah. Ray got called into work to help for a few hours, so I was poking around on the computer."

"I found something interesting in the diary of the latest victim." He told her about the rating system and the information about Bentley. And he added what he'd learned about the man from Seth.

"I'm seeing a pretty clear pattern here," she replied. "I asked one of the beat cops near his building if he'd ever run into him, and he told me something interesting. A few months ago, he and his partner broke up a tussle between Bentley and some chick. He had her arms pulled back and wouldn't let her leave. The chick had bruises on her wrists, but refused to press charges, so they had to let him go."

"He's the only person of interest we've found so far, so let's have a closer look. Did the other two still look clean?"

"As a whistle."

"Okay, give me the name of the beat cop you spoke to. I'll have a chat with him. Then I'll have another talk to Bentley." He paused. "I'm not tiring you out too much, am I?"

"Hell, no. You know me, I'd be goin' nuts with nothing to do."

"All right. That's what I thought. I'll call you later."

"Ciao."

It cracked him up to hear Sanchez say goodbye in Italian. Apparently, the proximity to Ray's family was having an effect.

****

Killing Alia March had given him a new appreciation for the perfect plan. Hey, if she was stupid enough to sit in a dark, almost empty parking lot, fiddling around instead of driving away, she deserved what she got. He'd strolled right up to her open window and shot her before she had the chance to look down her nose at him.

Temptation had beckoned, making him pause long enough to consider the possibilities. He would have loved to have screwed her as she died, to ensure that the last thing she saw was his face. The other choice would have been to pull her dress up and expose her like the whore she resembled. Speed was essential to these crimes, though—in and out with no one the wiser.

It was the key to his success along with insider knowledge. Smile at everyone and just hang in the background. You'd be surprised at the information you could glean from rambling conversations nobody knew you were overhearing.

Two clean kills almost made his bumble with the newscaster forgivable. And now, he got to go home and contemplate his ever-growing list of possible targets.

Lately, it was his favorite pastime.

****

First thing in the morning, Elijah had just sat down at his desk when his cellphone rang. He saw the call came from Pamela Clayton. Picking it up, he said, "Good morning. You're up early this morning."

"I don't have much time," she said, her lowered voice hard to hear with the clatter in the background. "I got an email last night from The Rhymester. I have to put it on the news because my boss insists, but I thought I'd give you fair warning. I'm sending it to you now."

After thanking her, he pulled up the email.

Alia Marks
I just can't believe how stupid women are
Sitting and waiting for death in their cars
For her vanity she paid a high price
Maybe she should have tried to be nice
The Rhymester

Elijah wondered, as he always did with serial killer cases, what had started this man on his journey of hate. Was it someone who'd never been successful with women as was so often the case? Statistically, people who showed this level of aggression toward women usually had either a sadistic mother figure or a lover who had humiliated them, sometimes both. While normal people would be hurt or depressed over such a thing and then get over it, troubled people often thought in terms of divine retribution. Thankfully, according to statistics, only a relative few then carried it out.

This killer longed for recognition, hence the poems. What else did he long for?

****

Sanchez heard the distinctive rattle of keys in the door and straightened, giving herself a tap on the face to wake herself up. Ray would only worry more if he knew she took a long nap in the afternoon to help regain her strength. "Hey, handsome," she teased as he poked his head through the open doorway. "How was your day?"

He sauntered across the room to drop a kiss on her lips. "It was a good news/bad news kinda thing. We finally caught the thief who's been stealing stuff. Unfortunately, it was everybody's favorite maid."

"Ah, jeez. You're kiddin'."

"Nope. She's been working for the hotel for almost ten years. The manager is going to let her make restitution, but she's out of a job." He plopped down on the sofa and pulled off his shoes with a groan, pausing to rub his feet. She chuckled at the gaping hole in his sock.

"Time for some new socks."

"Nah, Momma can sew it."

She faked an annoyed glower. "What, you're not going to ask me to do it?"

Grinning, he said, "I know better." He ducked the pillow that sailed across the room, aimed at his head. "Don't worry, babe. You have other amazing abilities. Speaking of which, what did you do for Elijah today?"

"Just hunting down some loose ends for him." She shifted and tugged the quilt over her legs. "What did you think of Dayle the other night?"

"Elijah's new squeeze? She seemed pretty nice. Smart, too. I guess she'd have to be to hang out with him." He recognized the concern on her face. "What, you don't like her?"

"It's not that. I like her okay."

"Then what's causing that furrow between your brows?"

She shrugged. "I don't know. He's just had shitty luck with women, that's all. Be nice if somethin' could work out for him in the long run. She better treat him right or she can answer to me."

"Just don't scare her off." He walked to the refrigerator and grabbed himself a beer, popping the cap. "Elijah's a big boy, despite your worries." He offered her a soda, but she nixed it. "I'm sure he can take care of his own love life."

"Well, jeez, nothing like statin' the obvious. It's just I know him. If it doesn't work out, he'll just shut himself in his house and read the rest of his life away."

"There are worse things than being a hermit. At least he's not the type to drink himself to death or worse."

"I don't know. I was pretty worried about him after

all the Cara Belton bullshit."

He shook his head. "That was just a short-term thing. Hazards of the job. All he needed was a boot in the ass which you so generously provided."

"He really needed it."

"I know that, and so does he."

"You ever go on one of those online dating deals?"

He looked surprised at her question. "Nah, I'm too old-fashioned for that stuff. How about you?"

"Hell, no. You can pretend to be anything or anyone on those kinds of sites. I was just looking into the one the victim joined. She made good use of it, but she was kissing a lot of toads along the way. And that site has a really good rating compared to most."

"Good thing we don't have to worry about that kind of stuff anymore, thank God." Glancing around the room, he said, "So where do you want to live after we get married?"

She looked at him like he had two heads. "What do you mean? We're gonna live here."

"I think we should look for a bigger place."

"How much room do two people need?"

"It's not always going to be just the two of us."

His words shocked her. They had talked about wanting kids, but always in general terms for the future. The idea suddenly stole their attention, front and center. Who was she kidding? She already had thirty-five long years behind her. Her sex drive would probably last until she reached a hundred, or at least she hoped it would, but the ability to carry children wouldn't.

"Don't freak out," he said, softening his tone. He moved to sit by her feet, his eyes full of love. "I'm just trying to think long term."

"I know, but are you sure we can afford a bigger place?"

"Sure. We both make decent money, and I've got some savings to spare. I don't mind if we have to spruce the place up a bit. The family will pitch in."

He made them sound like the mafia or something, but his father had been in construction and taught Ray his skills so that part didn't concern her. "Let's wait until after we get married, okay?"

"Sure, if you want." He twirled his empty bottle between his fingers. "When were you thinking we should get hitched?"

What, all of a sudden, they had to have their whole life planned out? "You in a big rush for some reason?" She raised her eyebrows.

He met her gaze and smiled. "Yes. I can't wait to be your husband."

She thought about getting stabbed and how she'd worried all the way to the hospital that she'd never see his goombah face ever again. Unaccustomed tears came to her eyes and, horrified, she ordered them away. Instead, she squeezed his hand. "And I can't wait to be your wife."

Chapter Eight

Elijah took a chance and walked a few blocks
north, pulling his jacket collar up against the wind. As
he hoped, he caught Patrolman George Vincent on his
beat and offered to buy him a coffee. He looked more
like a history teacher with his squat build and glasses,
but he gave a tentative smile. "I guess you talked to
your partner."

"Yes." He led him into the café next door and gave
his own order, waiting while the other man stated his
preference. The two black coffees appeared in an
instant, a curl of steam rising from both. Handing him
his cup and taking one for himself, they settled into a
nearby booth for a few minutes. "I'd appreciate
anything you could tell me about the altercation with
Bentley. The guy's name keeps popping up, and we
want to take a closer look."

He slurped and swallowed, rubbing one hand on
his pants. "Like I told Sanchez, I didn't like the way he
had her pinned against the car. Me and Harry hustled
right over. We got 'em separated, but then she said she
just wanted to leave. I tried to change her mind about
filing charges, but no go." He gritted his teeth. "The
bastard just smirked at us. He knew she was
embarrassed by the whole thing and didn't want to
attract any more attention."

"You didn't get her name?"

"You know, that's what I told Sanchez, but Harry remembered it the next day when I mentioned her call." He pulled a small coiled pad from his shirt pocket, flipping it open. "Catherine Peaks. I guess he checked her out in case she changed her mind. She owns a fancy antique store in the East End."

"That's great." He scrawled it in his notes. "You said he had her pinned. How? By the arms?"

"A wrist in each hand and pushed against the passenger door." He shook his head. "I hate that shit. Just the thought of any man trying to treat my sisters like that drives me nuts."

"Me, too. I'm planning to have a chat with her. I appreciate your time." The other man took a few more gulps of coffee and then, standing, returned to his beat.

Walking back to his car, Elijah decided to take a chance and try to catch Ms. Peaks at her store. It might be easier than trying to call her at home when she would be more likely to brush him off. He struggled to find a convenient parking spot nearby and ended up walking almost ten blocks. There were a lot of high-end restaurants and shops in this area which put parking at a premium. Still, it was nice to take a break and breathe some fresh air for a change. When he located her establishment, Peaks' Antiques, he stopped to enjoy his first impression. The front windows boasted some gorgeous Japanese Tansu chests, along with luminous vintage silks and glass vases. The latter sparkled in the sunlight that reached inside.

He let himself in through the reinforced door, noticing the security camera by the entrance. A soft musical tone announcing his arrival. In seconds, a woman appeared from behind the counter, dressed in a feminine pink suit and white ruffled blouse. According to the information he'd pulled up on his phone, she was in her early forties, but didn't look it. Her blonde hair was pulled back in an elegant chignon. As she approached, a professional smile crossed her face. "May I help you, or would you prefer to browse?"

Smiling, he walked up the aisle to greet her and pulled out his identification. "Detective Black, ma'am. Are you Ms. Catherine Peaks?"

"Yes. How can I help you?"

"I was wondering if I might have a few moments of your time."

Surprise parted her lips, then she recovered. "Of course. I believe I've seen you on the news, Detective. You're with the homicide division, aren't you?"

"Yes, ma'am. I wanted to ask you about a scuffle you had about six weeks ago with a man named Jarvis Bentley."

Elijah read embarrassment in her expression as her smile dimmed. "I didn't report that," she murmured.

"No, I know that. The beat cop on scene thought the encounter embarrassed you." He needed to put her at ease. "I can certainly understand that. I was wondering, though, if you could share with me the reason for your disagreement."

"Is this part of your case?"

"I'm sorry, ma'am. I'm not at liberty to say."

She gripped one hand with the other, glancing around to check for approaching customers. Sighing, she waved to two chairs by the sales desk. "Do you mind if we sit?"

"Not at all."

He waited until she was comfortable, then joined

her so that he sat in the opposite chair. "In retrospect, I probably should have pressed charges, but his sudden change in behavior shocked me." She ran a hand over the arm of her chair, her manicured nails gleaming. "We'd shared a lovely lunch, and he offered to see me to my car. I remember being pleased he was a gentleman. All of a sudden, he got quite physical."

"I know this is uncomfortable for you, but can you tell me exactly what he did?"

She nodded. "He grabbed me and tried to kiss me," she said as if forcing out the words from between her rigid lips. "I'm not used to such rough treatment, and I pulled away or at least tried to."

"Did you tell him no?"

"Y-yes, I did. Several times. It was as if he didn't hear me or, perhaps, chose not to hear me."

"So, he grabbed you. Did he restrain you?"

"Yes. He held my wrists and shoved me against the car."

"Anything else?"

She closed her eyes, bright color blossoming on her cheeks. "He rubbed himself against me and said, 'You know you want it.' " Tears appeared in the corners of her eyes as they inched open. "It appalled me. I felt helpless. After the two patrolmen intervened, I just wanted to go home and calm my nerves." She sucked in her breath. "I appreciated their help, I really did, but I just wanted to go home."

Spying a nearby box of tissues near the cash register, he stood, then handed them to her and resumed his seat. "I'm so sorry to upset you by bringing all of his terrible behavior up again."

She shook her head. "I've had more than enough

time to dwell on it, I'm afraid. I keep wondering what I should have done differently." Blotting the tears, she added, "I just couldn't believe I was so stupid. I should have seen it coming."

"Not necessarily. Predators come in all shapes and sizes." He met her gaze. "Did the incident leave you with bruises?"

She nodded. "I had to wear long-sleeved blouses for almost two weeks. That seemed easier than having to deal with awkward questions."

"I understand."

"Am I allowed to ask if he's done this kind of thing to anyone else?"

He chose his usual benign answer. "We're looking into that possibility. Thank you so much for your honest answers. I know it wasn't easy."

She attempted a smile. "Actually, I feel a little better having told someone. You have a very reassuring presence, Detective."

"Thank you, Ms. Peaks." He handed her one of his business cards. "If you should ever have any problems with him or any other man, please call. We have people in the department who can help."

"I'll do that." After bidding her goodbye, he held the door for two elderly women coming in and hoped they would distract the shop owner from her thoughts.

An unusual spurt of temper simmered as he walked back to his car. This guy's actions were reprehensible. How long had he been getting away with this kind of behavior? As of now, his name was going right to the top of their suspect list. The lives of rapists and murderers often started with lesser crimes.

Her predicament helped Elijah understand why he

had such a hard time in the dating world. In a lot of ways, he was an old-fashioned guy. He believed in good manners and had what Sanchez called 'protector syndrome.' It's one of the qualities which made him a good cop. But he also liked smart, independent women who had fulfilling careers and interests of their own. So often, women seemed to appreciate one side of him, but not the other.

His partner always teased him about being such a gentleman, but his parents had raised him that way. He'd been blessed with the best parents in the world and believed in the way he'd been brought up. Every day, some small memory of them would pass through his thoughts. He liked still living in the home he'd been raised in, surrounded by their pictures. If that made him sentimental, so be it.

It was part of the reason he was so proud of his partner. She'd been raised in what he called worst case scenario circumstances and still turned out to be a hard-working, caring person. She wasn't gushy and soft, but you couldn't find a kinder and more honest person. A lot of others would have used their difficult childhood as an excuse to whine or ask for handouts, but she had driven herself hard to excel at the police academy and prevailed.

He'd said those words to her before, and she'd rolled her eyes. He recognized her defense mechanisms for what they were and continued to treat her like a beloved sister.

After Cara's death, Sanchez had scraped him off the couch and made him start living again. She didn't understand why he'd cared so much about a serial killer, but she supported him anyway. That's the kind of friend he needed, and he treasured her.

He worked hour after hour on all the odds and ends of the case, learning nothing new. Now, night began to fall, the shadows creeping through his office blinds. He headed home.

The next morning, he dropped in to see his lieutenant and fill him in on the progress of the case. "Not much to work with, is it?" Sighing, Porter leaned back in his chair.

"No, sir, but there's a few threads to follow."

"Do you need some help with the computer stuff? I know that's not your favorite."

"Sanchez is bored stuck at home, so she offered to help." He saw the other man's concerned glance. "Don't worry. She promised to work for short spurts only, propped up on the couch."

"Okay, fine. How's she feeling?"

He chuckled. "She said her damn stitches are worse than the wound. They're itchy, I guess."

"Well, if that and boredom are her only complaints, I guess we're doing well." He tapped a pen on his desk, the resultant beat a familiar tune. "Do you need more assistance with this case?"

"I thought I might tag Jones in on some of the footwork if that's possible."

"Done. I'll have him shift a few of his cases. Do you want Hadley, too?"

Elijah tried to frame his words diplomatically, a struggle when it came to his least favorite co-worker. "I think Jones's help will be enough for now, sir."

"That's what I thought you'd say." He smiled. An intuitive man, he knew the score.

"I was wondering, sir, if you're familiar with

Officer Seth Parker?"

He nodded. "Big guy, brown hair, right? Been a patrolman for five, six years."

"Yes, that's him. I was wondering if you would have any issues with me encouraging him to take the detective's exam."

"No. I don't have any objections. Why him in particular?"

"He helped me with the Marks murder and did an excellent job. I asked around about him, and everything I heard was positive. We could use a few more like him; good work ethic and an eye for detail."

"We're always looking for hard-working men and women, you know that. By all means, have a chat and see if he's interested in writing the exam."

"Thank you, sir."

"Thanks for the update. Let me know if you need anything else."

He walked back to his office and made a note to talk to Seth. When Jones showed up at Elijah's desk thirty minutes later, he assigned him a small list of the endless follow throughs that happen with any case. He was no ball of fire, but he'd work through the list just fine.

Desperate for some fresh air, he left for a repeat interview with Bentley. It was a good thing he enjoyed the walk over, though, because the man had an appointment out of town for the day. The problem with wanting to surprise someone was that sometimes it backfired and proved to be a waste of time. Still, he couldn't deny that the same man dating two murder victims was statistically improbable. Given the additional incidences with Parker's sister and Ms.

Peaks, follow-up was essential.

Elijah spoke to Bentley's assistant and arranged for an appointment at nine a.m. the next day before heading back to the precinct. A visual person, he sat and stared at their white board for a long time. Pictures of the two victims were posted, along with the scant evidence they had accumulated thus far. Off to the side was a picture of Pamela Clayton and just the word Sanchez. He still had no idea if the cases were connected because of the difference in weapons. The timing made him suspicious. He would proceed as if they knew of a connection. It was the safest choice for everyone concerned.

Assailants tended to use knives when they wanted to get up close and personal. The average person didn't realize that knives were more dangerous than guns within a twelve-foot radius. Most people would be unable to carry out an accurate pistol shot that close up. There was simply not enough room to react and aim properly. But knives could kill you with one nasty swipe at that range.

Pamela Clayton fit the killer's type. She was an attractive, professional woman at the top of her field. Yes, she had fought him which had clearly caught him off guard, but without Sanchez's intervention she likely would have been killed.

It made sense to use a knife in those circumstances. It involved a lower noise level so the attacker could get in and out quickly with less chance of detection. That was the theory, anyway. He'd likely chosen the location because of the four exit doors he could access. The more he thought about it, the more certain he was that all three crimes involved the same culprit. Was it possible they could learn more from the women who'd survived rather than the scant evidence the deceased victims left behind?

After a few mouthfuls of coffee, he picked up his phone and called Sanchez. She answered after the first ring. "Hey, I was just going to call you."

"I have ESP," he teased. "You find anything interesting?"

"Yeah. Believe it or not, Clayton would give me a run for my money in the men department. Before Ray, I mean."

"That's really saying something."

"I know." She laughed. "She dated seven different guys just this month. Nothing wrong with it, of course. I'm actually kind of impressed. Anyway, haven't found much about any of them that raises any flags." A rustle of paper sounded over the line. "Now, Bentley's a little more interesting."

"In what way?"

"He makes a lot of money, right? He's a real hotshot. Nets a couple of million a year."

"The office space in that building doesn't come cheap, so I figured as much."

"Yeah, but I think he's spending more than he's making. I got a friend in the stock exchange who knows every damn body with big bucks. Just for giggles, I floated his name past him. When he said he knew him casually, I asked for an impression." Papers rattled again. "He said, and I'm quoting here, 'He's a bloodsucker and a fraud.' Apparently, his rich daddy paid for his firm's startup, his snazzy apartment, even his sportscar. He's a decent lawyer, but spending money is his favorite pastime, not practicing law."

"Unfortunately, that doesn't make him a killer."

"True, but it makes you wonder what else he's hiding. Did you have your second interview with him yet?"

He told her about the delay. Switching the subject, he asked, "Did you remember anything else about your attack?"

"No. I wish I could. I'd love to nail that sonofabitch."

"You and me both. Thanks for the information. You still feeling okay?"

"Yeah, bored and itchy. Same old, same old."

"All right. Say hi to Ray. We'll talk soon."

"Bye."

He thought long and hard about Jarvis Bentley and then forced himself back into the trenches.

****

The killer paced around his apartment, restless. He finally grabbed his favorite file and sat at his dining room table. Entrusting this information to a device would be foolhardy. Cellphones and computers could be easily hacked, and that was an unnecessary risk.

Opening the red manilla folder, blood red for inspiration, he spread the newspaper clippings, photos, and snippets of information out. The collection almost covered the tabletop. Two uppity women down and so many more to follow. Their traitorous faces smiled up at him.

They wouldn't be smiling for long.

The first bitch had been a restaurateur, the second a fashion designer. The potential targets left were a veritable smorgasbord of potential victims including a surgeon, a professor, even a judge. The latter made him laugh. Wouldn't it be fun if he killed someone he'd testified in front of? That might make the victory especially sweet.

They looked past him, these women, as if he was nothing but a smudge of dirt on their high-heeled shoes. Not just past him, but through him, as if he couldn't possibly prove worthy of their precious time. Sucking in a breath, he calmed himself. They were going to get their comeuppance. He just had to stay in control and plan everything out down to the last detail. Making mistakes could be fatal.

As much as he loved the idea of wielding his knife to get up close and personal, it hadn't worked as efficiently as he'd hoped. Using a gun had proven to be cleaner and easier; monthly practice made him an excellent shot.

Adding rape to the scenario would just have to stay in his fantasies.

For now.

Chapter Nine

Knowing he'd have to start the day off with another visit to Jarvis Bentley's office slowed Elijah's steps on the way to work. The painful truth made him clench his teeth. If a detective had to like the people he or she interviewed, they'd all be screwed. A lot of people were either scared of the police or determined to show defiance. Either scenario could end badly. Bentley just fell under the heading of arrogant as hell until proven otherwise.

At five minutes to nine, he settled once again in the waiting room, knowing he'd be forced to stay there past the appointed hour. Vain men needed their petty torments.

At nine-fifteen, the assistant accompanied him inside the door and departed, the aggressive click of her heels echoing back to him. Bentley gestured from his seat at the desk, not even bothering to rise this time. "Detective, come in and grab a seat. It's been a frantically busy morning. I'm sorry I'm running late." He didn't look remotely sorry. "Are you here about Ms. Bennett again?"

Elijah took more time than necessary getting settled in his seat, determined not to rush. Two could play this man's game. Pulling out his notebook, he flipped it open and pulled out a pen as the other man watched, gritting his teeth. "Actually, I'm here to ask you about Alia Parks."

"Oh, that's going to be a fun discussion." He rolled his eyes like a rebellious teenager.

Not a good look for any grown man. At least he knew better than to deny knowing her. "And why is that?"

"Because, to put it bluntly, she was a class A bitch. I don't mean to speak ill of the dead, but—"

"Yet, you seem to be doing exactly that."

He shoved forward, setting his forearms against the edge of his desk. "I just meant that she was a real ballbuster. I wish I'd never wasted my precious time on her."

"How many times did you go out with her?"

The gleaming teeth disappeared as he frowned. "Three times. In her case, the third time was definitely not the charm."

"What happened on that third date?" He knew, of course, thanks to Alia Marks's diary. He just wondered if he would admit to insisting she pay half the check. And didn't he realize that maligning a woman who'd just died didn't leave a positive impression?

"She lost her temper about a small difference of opinion about our food and stormed out of the restaurant. It wasted my entire evening, not to mention a great deal of money."

He nodded in what he hoped looked like an understanding way. "And you didn't call her again?"

"Absolutely not. I sent her a curt email to signal my displeasure." He lifted his chin, offering a snapshot of his usual arrogance. "I have a long list of women to select from, Detective. Any random choice would be a better use of my free time."

"Were you aware that Ms. Parks used a rating system for her lovers?"

A flicker of annoyance crossed his face, but then a smirk replaced it. "She wouldn't be the only one."

Did he really think that his using one would be a surprise to anyone who knew him? "Have you ever seen her ratings?"

"No."

Elijah smiled. "Apparently, she wasn't particularly impressed with you, either." He took note of his angry expression and didn't give him a chance to reply. "Can you tell me where you were between the hours of midnight and two a.m. on last Saturday morning, the twentieth?"

"Certainly. In bed, as always. I need my beauty sleep."

"Were you alone?"

He smiled. "Actually, two female friends were with me from about ten until two, so I guess I'm covered." A smug smile crossed his face. "In more ways than one if you get my drift."

Did he have to pay them to stick around, he wondered? He couldn't imagine another reason they'd be with him. No money in the world is worth putting up with that inflated ego. "If you can provide me with their names, I'd appreciate it."

"Of course." He looked them up on his phone, made a note, and handed it across the desk.

Time to rattle his cage a little. "Do you know a woman named Catherine Peaks?"

His eyes narrowed. "We've had lunch a time or two. She's not connected to this case, is she?"

"No, she's not. But, because of this case, we're just

keeping an eye on any reports of aggressive behavior toward women. I'm sure you understand why we'd be concerned." Meeting his gaze to get his point across, he rose. "Thank you for your time."

The other man grunted a response and, pleased he'd caught him off guard, Elijah left.

****

Midweek, Elijah texted Dayle.

—Any chance you're free for dinner on Friday?—

—Yes, I'm available. Where would you like to go?—

—I thought maybe takeout and a movie at my place. What do you think? You can choose both.—

It took her some time to get back to him, and he worried he'd been too forward and scared her off. Then she finally answered.

—Sorry. Got interrupted. How about Chinese food? Any movies except horror or politics.—

—Perfect. Seven o'clock?—

—Text me your address and I'll see you then.—

Her response gave him a much-needed jolt of energy. He would work every hour possible for the next two days to earn the hours off with her. With a little luck, they wouldn't get interrupted and he could get to know her better.

Doomed to disappointment, he discovered that Bentley didn't have any registered guns. It was hardly difficult to purchase one almost anywhere these days, but there was no way to prove it. Still, he'd keep an eye on him and keep digging.

****

It was a good thing Elijah was so busy at work, because unexpected nerves plagued him on Friday.

Thankfully, he was a tidy person by nature, so there would be no last-minute dashing around to scrub the bathrooms and vacuum.

Still, having something to do might have helped distract him as he waited for Dayle to arrive. Emerging an hour earlier from his favorite Chinese takeout, his arms laden, he knew he'd bought way too much food. It didn't matter because he could freeze leftovers. Making sure Dayle got what she wanted was important to him. He had both white and red wine waiting.

He wore his usual khakis and a plain white cotton button down shirt. When the front bell finally rang, he hurried to open the door. She stood, smiling, on the stoop, a bakery box of cookies in her hand. "Welcome. You found the address without any trouble?"

"Yes."

He waved her inside before taking the box and her jacket. Her outfit made him smile. The beige slacks and white blouse were the female version of his own outfit. He gestured from one to the other. "Great minds, I guess. New York casual."

She laughed, and the low tone of it appealed to him. Following him into the kitchen, she looked around and said, "What a beautiful home. I expected an apartment like mine."

"I inherited it from my parents."

"Lucky you. These old brownstones are such a treasure." She indicated she would prefer white wine, and he poured her a glass. Thanking him, she picked it up and turned to wander toward a side table full of photographs. "Are these your parents?"

"Yes."

"They look bursting with pride as they should be."

She looked at his academy graduation photograph. "What made you decide to be a policeman?"

He lifted his glass toward her in a small toast. "A rather naïve belief that I could make a difference."

"From the coverage I've read, you certainly have."

He smiled. "Don't believe everything you read. I can't say interacting with the media has been much fun. They have to do their job, of course, but it doesn't make mine much easier."

She frowned. "Or mine. I'm always paranoid I'll say the wrong word and they'll be ready to jump. Blowing things out of proportion seems to be a fulltime occupation for them."

"How did you decide to become a lawyer?"

"My mother would say that I showed an early aptitude for arguing."

He laughed. "An essential skill in your line of work."

"For whatever reason, I have a deeply engrained sense of justice. I want to try and ensure the good guys always win."

"That's one thing we have in common."

She took a sip of wine, then turned to face him. "Do you date very much?"

Her blunt question surprised him, but he preferred her being forthright. "I don't, actually. Time has an unfortunate habit of slipping away from me." He moved to the couch and waited for her to join him before sitting. "How about you?"

"The same, I guess. Our careers are both demanding. Any spare time I can get frequently goes to catching up on sleep."

A passing image of her sleeping in his bed flirted

with him, and he pushed the distracting thought away. "I agree. I'm trying to do better with my life outside work, though, in case you haven't guessed."

"Is that why you asked me out?"

"It's one of the reasons. Add in that you're an attractive, intelligent woman and it's an easy decision." He smiled. "I was both surprised and relieved that I didn't have to stand in line."

She flushed, the color giving life to her pale cheeks. "I've been told I can be rather unapproachable."

He hadn't found that at all. "That surprises me. I found you very easy to approach. But I've been accused of the same thing, so perhaps it's just a case of like recognizing like."

"Maybe so." She glanced around the room. "Your antiques are beautiful."

"Thank you. My mother loved to hunt down neglected pieces at estate sales. She and my father would lug them down to his workroom, then sand and stain them back to life."

"The décor is beautiful, but warm and homey, too. I like that. Your parents had a wonderful eye for interior design." She met his gaze. "Were you born here in the city?"

He laughed. "Right in this house, actually. My parents didn't quite make it to the hospital. The story is a bit of a neighborhood legend."

"Oh, your poor mother. She must have been frightened."

"Actually, she used to joke that she just wanted to save money."

The shock on her face was followed by humor. "I'm not sure I'd choose that path to avoid hospital bills."

"It's a fun story, though. I came roaring into the world surrounded by my grandparents, neighbors, and a few friends. A doctor summoned from a few blocks away arrived just in time to cut the cord. Everyone agreed I was just so big that I ran out of room and demanded an exit."

They both chuckled. "How about your parents?" he asked.

A shadow came over her face. "Not as happy a story, I'm afraid. My father abandoned us when I was ten. My mother lives upstate with my stepfather."

He regretted asking because the light had gone from her eyes. "I'm sorry, Dayle."

"It's fine." She glanced into the kitchen. "So, what goodies did you find for dinner?"

He recognized her need to change the subject and led the way back into the kitchen. There would be another time to learn her personal history. Opening the refrigerator, he let her look at the multitude of colorful containers that waited inside. Tempting aromas wafted out.

Raising her eyebrows, she said, "I guess the more succinct question would be what didn't you find. That seems like a lot of food for two people."

He moved the containers onto the oversized granite island so she could see everything. "I bought sweet and sour chicken, beef chow mien, snow peas and water chestnuts, egg drop soup, sweet and sour soup, eggrolls, and fortune cookies." He grinned. "Never shop when you're hungry. I hardly eat at all while I'm working, but then I make up for it."

"I won't eat again for days."

"Show me what you want to start with, and I'll load up your plate." He opened a nearby cabinet and lay two plates on the countertop along with silverware and napkins.

Dayle reached across and took one of her implements. "I can take care of mine. You get yours, then we'll microwave them." She filled hers and set it in the microwave. Turning it on caused the requisite hum as it heated. "Do you like to cook?"

"I'm afraid not. Do you?"

"Actually, I'm trying to teach myself with the help of social media and a few good cookbooks. I get tired of restaurants and takeout. I was just thinking that this beautiful kitchen is wasted on you."

He thought about the gourmet appliances and sprawling granite island his mother had designed. "The year my mother died, she insisted on my updating the kitchen. I think it gave her a sense of peace to leave both the house and me in as sound condition as she could."

"That's so sweet."

They carried the plates to the polished mahogany table in the attached dining room. "What kind of movies do you like best?" he asked.

"Mysteries or comedies."

"Do you like vintage movies? I was thinking maybe Rear Window."

"Oh, I'd love to watch that. I haven't seen it in years."

Pulling out the sliding shelf, he selected the DVD they wanted. She made a comment about how many movies he owned, and he laughed. "Actually, I have four more drawers like this one. I'm a homebody."

Selecting the chosen film, he put on the DVD. They made themselves comfortable, sitting down to eat and watch the film. When they were finished eating, he took a minute to scrape the plates and put away the leftovers, then they moved to the couch. At the scariest part, she grabbed his hand, not seeming to notice. The simple heat of her soft skin warmed him.

Her hair smelled like blackberries. He wanted to touch the shining strands, but it seemed too forward. It had been far too long since he enjoyed a woman's company. *Don't get distracted.* He forced his attention back to the movie.

After it was over, she turned to him, the edges of her lips curled in a smile. It was so natural for him to lean and kiss her, taking his time in case she wanted to retreat. She met him halfway, though, leaning into him. Now, he touched his fingers to her hair and stroked.

Heat and a sense of connection were there in her eager response. He sensed it was just enough for tonight and ended the kiss. "I'm so glad you came tonight."

"Me, too." She leaned back and slipped her hand away. "I should probably head out. I have casework to catch up on tomorrow." After she stood, she said, "I forgot to ask how your case was going."

"More slowly than I would like. We're muddling through some clues."

"That's frustrating."

"Yes, it is." When he realized she'd taken a cab, he offered to drive her home.

"Don't be silly," she said, sliding on her jacket. She tapped a message into her phone and got an immediate response. "He'll be here in five minutes." Putting a hand on his arm, she continued, "I'll let you walk me out, though, and keep me company until he arrives."

Throwing on his jacket, he did so, stopping at the curb. He clasped her hands as they waited. A few of the neighborhood's teenage boys wandered by, offering hearty wolf whistles that strained their ear drums. "Sorry about that."

She smiled. "If over-sexed teenagers were all I had to worry about, life would be simple."

The cab appeared, too soon, speeding down the street and pulling up right in front of them. She reached up to brush his cheek with her lips, then he opened the door and handed her inside. "Goodnight."

"Goodnight, Elijah."

He stood as the car disappeared from sight, watching her departure like some lovestruck kid. As far as second dates went, it couldn't have gone any better.

He just hoped she felt the same way.

Chapter Ten

The Rhymester picked his next victim just because she was chosen to host a series of talks about the power of women. *What a bunch of claptrap.* A bitch encouraging other bitches to become even more delusional than they already were. *Terrific.*

Women in the workplace, my ass, he thought, smashing his glass beer mug against the table's edge. The handle snapped off in his hand. A few dots of blood dripped from his fingers. *Damn it.* Now, see what they'd done. That had been his favorite mug.

The first presentation took place next Wednesday night at the university closest to his house. An evil plan brewed. Wouldn't it be fitting if he killed her going to the talk? Or, even better, right after she'd finished when she was distracted by the undeserved applause ringing in her ears. He could envision it, and it made him smile.

He would have to get to work immediately, learning her habits. If he was careful, he could do some of that during work hours. There wasn't much time to prepare, but this target seemed like the right choice. And maybe, just maybe, he could find a way to involve Pamela Clayton and make it a 'two birds, one stone' kind of thing.

Then, he'd get a hell of a lot of media coverage, wouldn't he? The recognition, finally, that he so richly deserved. He glanced up at the worn dartboard on the opposite wall of his bedroom. The entire surface was covered by faces of women, including his ex-wife. Picking up a dart, he grinned and let it fly.

Bullseye.

****

Dayle thought about Elijah as she got ready for bed, a welcome heat stealing over her body. It had been a depressingly long time since spending time with any man excited her. Excited in all of the right ways, from her head to her reluctant heart and beyond. He had to have flaws, everyone did, but they weren't readily apparent. There were no big, glaring red flags that warned her to run in the opposite direction.

When he'd kissed her, he'd allowed her the opportunity to back off if she wanted to, but she hadn't. His soft, firm lips had tempted her just enough to sense there was much more to come. Would he carry that same focused attention into the bedroom?

She certainly hoped so. Her body had responded in a way she'd almost forgotten it could.

Settling for an average relationship didn't suit her. Doing that in her first marriage was her deepest regret. She'd been lonely and looking for lasting companionship. Her ex-husband's caveman behavior had forever cured her of putting up with abusers. She had paid dearly for making a disastrous choice.

She carried the seductive thoughts about Elijah to bed, having satisfying dreams for a change. If compelling dreams translated to reality, she'd have a lot more enjoyment in store.

On Tuesday night, she took a few hours to herself after work and looked into a volunteering opportunity. One of the local women's shelters was searching for some career women who could help their clients re-enter the professional world. The general idea was to persuade local vendors to commit free clothing, beauty treatments, and other image enhancers to help those who were looking for a fresh start. She could do that. She knew how to elicit a positive response, a necessity in her job.

Locating the old, brick building had been easy with the help of a friendly cab driver. The manager, Sara Towers, met her at the door, welcoming her. She had just begun a guided tour of the facility when, turning a corner, they almost bumped into Elijah. An unexpected flush of pleasure came over her. "Hi. What are you doing here?"

He smiled, the gesture lighting his eyes. "I was about to ask you the same thing."

Sara said, "Oh, you two know each other." She smiled. "Detective Black is considering awarding us some private funding." Turning toward him, she added, "And Ms. Stockard is interested in helping the transition team for our clients who want to re-enter the professional world." Pausing, she looked back and forth between the two of them. "Would you like to take the rest of the tour together?"

They both agreed and followed her first into the large playroom. A large, older model television sat in one cramped corner, framed by worn wooden shelves packed with toys and games. Children gathered in small groups, playing board games he recognized from his youth. They looked up at the adults, their faces latching onto Mrs. Towers for reassurance, but clearly wary about their presence.

She smiled to calm them, then lowered her voice.

"This is one of the rooms we'd like to update. We currently have to use it as a school area as well, and there's definitely room for improvement." Walking to the other end, which was empty, she said, "We have enough space here for desks, shelves, and a few computers, but we currently lack the resources. Our plan is to stress that education can be a road out of their current situation."

They ventured down a long hall and made their way to the kitchen. Although it was a spacious room with good light from several large windows, the older appliances appeared to be on their last legs. "The basics are here for a good setup," Dayle said, trying to be positive.

The other woman nodded. "I agree. The appliances, though, are running on borrowed time. Replacing all of them would be very expensive. And we could save more money on groceries if we had a freezer."

Elijah stared at the long, bare wall on the opposite side from the appliances, his eyes narrowed. "Where does everyone eat?"

"In the playroom."

"So, the playroom does triple duty—play, school, and dining?"

"Yes." She smiled. Dayle realized how tired she looked, with dark shadows around her eyes. "It's not ideal, but we make it work."

He paused, and she could tell he was calculating. "What if you built a long, farm style table along that wall with shelving overhead? It wouldn't cost much, but then the children, at least, would have somewhere more comfortable to eat."

She sighed. "In a perfect world, we could have that, too, but we have more pressing priorities. There are always necessities battling with desires." Nodding, he took a small pad from his pocket and made a few notes.

Their final stop was to the bedroom hall. As Dayle trailed the other two inside, she brushed a tear from her eye. The few women who sat on the beds looked frightened when they saw Elijah. Mrs. Towers explained that he was a policeman, but her assurance didn't seem to help calm them. The shelter staff had tried to do their best with the available funds, but the room depressed Dayle. The mismatched beds looked to be in poor repair, the bedcovers worn. The drab, gray walls lent credence to the need for change. "How many families stay here on a regular basis?" she asked.

"We can help twenty families, but that's at maximum capacity." She frowned. "Sadly, we have to turn away people all the time which breaks my heart."

"Have you seen everything you want to see?" he asked Dayle, compassion in his gaze.

"Yes." She smiled to reassure him.

He turned to the other woman. "Is it all right if we talk in your office? And may Dayle join us?"

"Of course." Mrs. Towers bustled down the hall to a tiny, crowded office. "I'm sorry it's so small. I hate to take any space away from the families." She sat behind her scarred desk to leave barely enough room for the two of them to take a seat on the remaining chairs. "Is there anything else I can tell you or show you to help make your decision easier?"

He waited until Dayle sat before taking his own seat. "Yes. If you could have an assistant, would that be of help to you?"

A wistful smile appeared. "Oh, that would be wonderful, but I don't see it ever happening. As you know, our list of needs is long. Squeaking by with minimal staff means more food on the table for everyone. It's a question of priorities."

"How many hours a week are you currently working?"

Both guilt and fatigue showed in her eyes. "About seventy. Sometimes my husband comes to help me out so we can spend more time together. I try to keep it to fewer hours, but it's hard to say no when there's so many families in need."

The poor woman. It must be exhausting. She worked long hours, too, but the work wasn't so emotionally draining. She stayed silent, letting Elijah continue.

"I understand. I must say I was very impressed by how far you've managed to stretch your current funding. That can't be easy."

Her expression lightened. "Thank you, Detective Black. I've become quite adept at sniffing out deals."

He smiled. "You can call me Elijah. I think we're going to be seeing a lot more of each other in the coming months."

She paused, then looked back and forth between the two of them, an expression of hope blooming on her face. "Do you mean—"

"I mean that it's clear the items on your wish list are both reasonable and necessary for the future of this facility. I am going to give you and your board the entire amount you requested."

She burst into tears. Elijah looked at Dayle,

panicked eyes signaling his need for assistance. Understanding that he didn't know what to do, she stood to hug the other woman. "It's wonderful news," she murmured, feeling the woman's shoulders shake with emotion.

After a moment, she pulled away, wiping her eyes. "Oh, my goodness, I'm so sorry. I'm a little over-tired, I'm afraid." She reached forward to take his hand in hers. "Thank you so much, Elijah. You can't possibly know what your generosity means to us."

"You're welcome. If you like, we can find some volunteers at our precinct to help paint and build a few things. That would mean we could afford to add the table in the kitchen and storage as well. And I have a few ideas about how to design a better floorplan for the sleeping areas."

"I would love to hear all of your ideas," she said. "I'm kind of a jack of all trades around here, and I can always use another perspective. And having extra pairs of hands to help would be an incredible blessing."

"Good. I also think we can eventually cover the cost of an assistant as well, but we'll get started on the other things first." He stood, glancing at his watch. "I'll let you inform your board members. If you give me your banking information, I'll have the amount transferred within the next few days. In the meantime, we should head out, so you can get everyone settled down for the night."

"I'll email the bank information first thing in the morning." She followed them, her smile beaming, to the door. After they said goodnight, she closed the door behind them. Right after, they heard the slide and snap of a heavy bolt. Dayle turned and hugged Elijah. She could feel his surprise, then his arms closed around her. "That was more emotional than expected," he murmured.

"Those poor people." She pulled away to look up at him. "It makes you realize just how lucky we are."

"Yes. Next time I complain, feel free to lecture me."

"As long as you do the same to me." They walked down the driveway. "It must be wonderful to be able to help people like that."

"It's my first time. Even though it's not really my money, I enjoyed helping."

"Not your money?"

He shrugged. "It was entrusted to me for the specific purpose of helping people in this situation. I don't consider it mine."

How many men would give away that kind of cash? She'd heard rumors it was millions. "You're a kind and generous man."

"I try to be. I've been incredibly lucky in my life to have the family I did. It's nice to help others who haven't had it so easy." When they reached the sidewalk, he paused. "Did you take a cab?"

"Yes."

"I have my car. Let me drive you home."

"Thank you. I'd like that."

They spoke more about his ideas on how to improve the center and, before she knew it, they arrived at her door. She leaned over and kissed him. This time, even more, she felt the building heat as her chest rubbed against him. Not the time or the place, she thought with disappointment, pulling away. Reaching a hand up, she stroked his cheek. "Goodnight, Elijah."

Chapter Eleven

Elijah thought about the way her body fit against his all the way home. Their chemistry held promise. It had been all he could do not to just keep driving and take her back to his bed. But he wanted their first time together to be perfect. What that might look like was something he should consider. The promise of sexual pleasure loomed.

It would give him joy to give those funds to the shelter. He hadn't realized just how wonderful it would feel to make such a big difference to a great cause. If he and Dayle could share an interest in those causes, too, that would give them another interest in common.

Attraction, work, and a common goal made a great place to start a relationship. And, the shocking thing was, he knew that's what it would be already. This wasn't going to be a flash in the pan thing, he and Dayle. Their connection had been apparent from the first moment they'd spoken.

Once at home, he had a big glass of water and went to bed. Hopefully, he'd get lucky and sleep through the night with only pleasant dreams to enjoy.

In the morning, he was working on case details at the office when something occurred to him. Right before Sylvia Bennett had been murdered, she had been featured in a local magazine as a successful entrepreneur. The article had come to light during their research.

Digging through the information on the second victim revealed a recent fashion article in one of the newspapers about her. It made him wonder if this was the method by which their killer chose his victims. He picked up his cellphone and called Sanchez. "Yo," she answered. "Thought you forgot about me."

"I wouldn't dare. Thought I'd let you know that I noticed something interesting. Before their deaths, both the first victim and the second had an article published about them."

"Yeah? Where?"

"The first in a magazine, the second in the newspaper. Can you find out whether Pamela had something similar written about her lately? If so, that might be the evidence we need to tie your attack to the murders."

"You figure that's how he's picking his victims?"

"I hope so. If so, that would also give us a leg up on who he might hit next."

"Okay. Let me do a search. If I can't find anything, I'll track her down and ask her."

"Thanks."

Ten minutes later, she was back on the phone. "Your instincts were right on the mark. Six days before the attack on her, she had this blurb in the paper. Top crime reporter of the year or some such bullshit." He heard the crinkle of paper followed by chewing sounds and knew she was eating a candy bar. "First solid lead, bud. Good work."

"Thanks. When is the doctor letting you come back?"

"Next Monday."

"Better than nothing. We miss you."

"Boo-hoo, you big softie."

"Bye."

He went over to his lieutenant's office and filled him in on the encouraging news. "I'll make a list of prominent women recently featured in local magazines and papers to see if we can narrow down possible targets."

"I hope you're right. We could use a break." He urged him to continue pursuing that line of enquiry and waved him out.

The afternoon fled as he compiled a list of seven names that he thought could be possible targets. All were female high achievers in various industries who had recently received attention in the press. Working on how spaced out the attacks had been, he knew they were close to due for another one. Knowing that made him twitch with frustration.

He scanned through the articles, and the bottom paragraph of one of the pages caught his eye. One of the women, Audrey King, was speaking at the local university tonight at seven o'clock. He glanced at his watch. The program had just started. An odd premonition crept up his spine when read the title of her presentation—Women at the Forefront.

Paranoia had him grabbing his jacket and checking his weapon. The nearby campus meant he could be there in twenty minutes. Considering the subject matter convinced him to take the time to check it out. The title of the talk alone might anger their killer enough to make an appearance. If everything appeared quiet as the speaker exited the building and made her way to her car, he could just go home from there with no one the wiser. He trusted his instincts, though. Wouldn't these talks be just the kind of thing that would yank this killer's chain?

He hurried down the stairwell to the crowded garage to get his car. As he climbed in and started the engine, he considered the details. University security was always quite dismal with too many dark corners for barely trained security guards to cover. If most people read the rape statistics on all universities, no female child would ever be allowed to attend.

But murder? He couldn't call for backup based on a hunch, but protecting one woman in a crowd would be impossible. It made more sense that the killer might try to single her out, maybe in the parking lot. As he sped along quieter side streets, he wished he knew where the speaker had parked her car. He wasn't familiar enough with the university grounds to remember the layout around those buildings, but there would be multiple parking areas.

Most presentations of that type lasted an hour, more or less. Were they having dinner beforehand? He didn't know. The article hadn't mentioned many details, just the time and place.

The parking guard gave Elijah a decent parking spot in the largest lot close to the building after he flashed his badge. He glanced around as he pulled into the narrow spot, hoping this was where she would have parked, too. Open on three sides, the lot's fourth side had a thick swath of trees. He could observe the entire open area with no problem from any place close to the building.

He turned and headed for the location. Walking along the shadowed approach, he saw the large front entrance and guessed that she would likely exit there rather than from a side door. Most of the parking spots were more convenient from that location. *Good.* That helped narrow the possible approaches he could make and still stay somewhat hidden from sight.

Pausing under a streetlight, he peered again at the speaker's picture posted near the front steps. Audrey King was a top-selling local realtor, an attractive black woman, tall and well-dressed.

Seeing no one skulking around outside, he went inside, glancing at his watch. Elijah located the theatre where the talk was being held. If they'd started on time, they'd been at it for an hour. He peeked through the window set into the door and saw her on stage. Her charismatic voice rang out. Judging by the chuckles he could hear, she was an amusing speaker.

He checked the adjacent halls, glancing into empty rooms, and saw nothing to alarm him. A janitor in a drab beige uniform swept the floor as a few people walked by, clearly heading somewhere else. Ear buds in his ears, he nodded his head to unheard music as he worked. Stationing himself just down the hall, Elijah realized he would hear the applause when Mrs. King finished her presentation. According to the hall poster, she was the only speaker tonight. That meant she would likely leave soon after the talk ended. He could simply trail her out with the rest of the departing crowd and ensure she made it safely to her car.

If he was the assailant, he'd plan to shoot her in the parking lot where she would be a solitary target, away from others and in dimmer light. Killers always chose the place where a target was the most vulnerable. Even though lots were usually dark and somewhat empty at times, people behaved carelessly in them. They were often tired and just wanted to get home after a long day.

It would be great if he was wrong. If so, he could just go home and sleep, a much safer option.

Ten minutes later, he heard prolonged applause and prepared himself. First, a bustling crowd of women left, chatting happily amongst themselves. After a few moments, Mrs. King appeared, staff members wearing identification badges clustered around her. The sole woman who seemed to be in charge thanked her as they walked down the long hall together. Now, there were no men to be seen other than him.

He stayed twenty paces behind her as she exited, ignoring the few casual glances that came his way. She paused outside to say her final goodbyes, then headed down the steps, striding with confidence toward the main lot.

Most women were staying to chat a little longer which allowed him better line of sight. Scanning the thick grove of nearby trees that would provide the only cover, he kept moving. He sidled a little closer to her, staying to the opposite side of the lot to keep a wide area in view.

He scanned his surroundings. At first, nothing caught his eye. A blur of movement darting from the trees was his only warning. A tall, dark figure with a stocky build ran silently in her direction, his approaching steps cushioned by the thick grass.

"Get down," Elijah yelled before sprinting across the stretch of asphalt to intercept the line of fire. The other man's arm reached out, the outline of the gun a clear silhouette under the streetlights. Elijah saw a flash of color as Mrs. King ducked down behind a car.

Foiled, the killer swung away from her, toward him, and shot. He fired in response, the shot booming in the near silence. A grunt told him he'd hit the attacker who took a stumbling step, then whirled and ran in the opposite direction toward cover.

With distant shrieks filling his ears, he gave chase as the man disappeared into the trees. Pain in his left arm told him he'd been hit by a glancing shot. Under the canopy of branches, he saw there were too many ways for the shooter to escape. Coming to a halt, he listened for the sound of running steps.

Damn it. Nothing.

A few moments more of searching confirmed the shooter had managed to escape. Elijah called the incident in to his precinct, describing the shooter and requesting assistance. Frustrated, he returned to the lot where Mrs. King waited, surrounded now by shocked staff and others. A woman screamed as he approached, and he lifted his badge, turning it for all to see. "Detective Black. Are you okay, Mrs. King?"

"Y-yes, I think so." She took a shaky step toward him, reaching a hand out. "Detective, you're bleeding."

"It's okay, ma'am. It's looks worse than it is."

"Who should we call?" a bystander asked, the buzz of the crowd increasing in volume.

He turned and raised his voice to be heard by the entire crowd. "Help is on the way. If you could stay where you are, we'd like to interview everyone who was in the vicinity."

The rising racket of excitement meant they would. Sirens could be heard wailing in the distance, probably mere moments away. Walking a few steps toward the intended victim, he ignored the cellphones raised to take pictures. Women had banded around the speaker as she stood, her arms wrapped around herself for comfort. She looked up at him, disbelief causing lines of concern on her face. "Was that man really shooting at me?"

"Yes, ma'am. I'm sorry. We'll explain more down at the precinct. I'm afraid you'll have to come and make a statement." His heartbeat finally started to slow, the surge of adrenaline fading. "Is there anyone you should call? There will be news cameras showing up at any moment, and I don't want your family to worry."

"My husband." She shivered. He took off his jacket, placing it around her shoulders.

"Call him now." He smiled. "Your first sentence should be, 'I'm fine, and I have a policeman with me.' "

A faint smile appeared. "Good thinking. Anton does worry." Straightening her shoulders with resolve, she removed a cellphone from her purse with trembling hands and punched in a number. Her sense of calm despite the frightening situation impressed him.

As she finished her call, he saw four patrol cars and an ambulance racing down the drive, lights rotating. Cutting their sirens as they came to a stop lowered the noise level. They pulled into the lot to park helter-skelter, and he walked toward them, his shield held out for all to see. Most would know him, but he wasn't taking any chances at having a rookie take a potshot. Five minutes later, the officers and emergency medical technicians had been apprised of the details and got down to work.

One group sectioned off to interview the members of the crowd. Another put up crime tape. Crime scene technicians searched for any evidence which might help. The medical staff dressed his wound, a shallow gouge that caused more blood than damage. He'd been lucky. He had them check Mrs. King for shock, just to be on the safe side. They replaced his jacket with a blanket to be certain she stayed warm and returned it to him.

When the basic necessities were taken care of, he surrendered his gun to his lieutenant and gave him a quick rundown of the attack. This was protocol in the event of a cop related shooting. His boss drove Mrs. King to the precinct, and he followed in his own car. As they arrived inside, a distraught older man rushed up, calling the intended victim by her first name. "Her husband," Elijah announced to calm the others as he grabbed her and hugged her. She patted his back, murmuring, "I'm okay, honey. Everything's fine. Don't worry."

He peered at Elijah, eyeing his bandaged arm. "Are you the man who saved her?"

Nodding, he said, "Detective Black," reaching out a hand to shake.

The other man pumped it with vigor. "I can never repay you for your actions on my wife's behalf."

"Happy to help, sir. It's my job." He smiled. "Come with us. I think we could all use a cup of coffee." They filed into one of the conference rooms rather than cram everyone into a smaller office. Mrs. King was taken to one end of the massive table to give her statement. He stayed at the other to keep her husband company.

"Am I allowed to ask questions?" Mr. King met his gaze, the lines of strain finally softening.

"You can certainly ask whatever questions you like. I may or may not be able to answer because of our current investigation."

"Understood." He took a moment as if trying to muddle through his scattered thoughts. "Did you just happen to be in the same area as Audrey?"

He couldn't see any reason he couldn't tell him that. "As strange as it probably sounds, I simply followed a hunch." Explaining about the article took a moment. "I would appreciate if you could keep that to yourself."

"Of course. I'm so grateful you followed your instincts." His hands were trembling, so he cradled one in the other and held them in his lap. "I'm almost scared to ask. Does this have anything to do with the previous killings of the two other professional women? The ones that have been in the news?"

"I'm afraid I can't answer that, sir. At this point, everything is conjecture." He smiled. "I do have a piece of advice for you in the coming days."

"What's that?"

"Don't talk to the press. It will just feed the frenzy. Lay low for the next few days, and the manic fight for your wife's story should slow down."

The other man met his gaze, his expression sober. "I'm afraid I've done you a disservice, Detective."

The comment confused him. "How so, sir?"

"When I saw you on the evening news the other day, I called you a showboat. Told my wife you should be working the case, not posing for pictures." He grimaced. "Given tonight's attack on my wife, I truly regret my careless words."

"Don't worry about it." He leaned closer, lowering his voice. "I hate those press briefings more than you could ever know. Unfortunately, it's part of the job."

A short while later, Mrs. King was released. He arranged for the couple to have an escort home and for two patrolmen to park in front of her house for the time being. They would help control the inevitable crowds of news people and keep an eye out for their safety until things died down.

It was 2:30 a.m. when the lieutenant moved to slump into the chair next to him. "I'm getting too old for this crap."

"Sorry for delaying your sleep, sir."

"I'd give a million bucks for your instincts, Elijah."

The use of his first name surprised him. Last names were standard in every police department. He took it as a compliment. "I realized each of the woman had an article written about them recently. After digging around, she was on the short list of women who had been interviewed. We were damn lucky they listed the upcoming event in the article. I honestly thought I was being paranoid."

"Keep being paranoid. If it means we can save a life, all the drama is more than worth it." He sighed. "Can you run the facts of the shooting by me once more while they're fresh in your mind?"

Elijah did as he asked as briefly as possible.

"Okay, thanks." His boss stood, groaning, as he stretched his back out. "Let's go home and grab a few hours sack time. I'll make sure the shooting team does your interview about the incident first thing, so they'll return your gun and you can get back to work."

"Appreciate that, sir."

After his boss left, he decided to sleep at the precinct. Years ago, he'd learned to keep fresh clothes at work. He grabbed a shower and slept for almost four hours in the off-duty room. At seven, he woke and replaced his bandage from items nabbed from the first aid kit. With fresh clothes and some sleep behind him, he prepared for another hectic day.

His phone blew up with calls and texts as soon as the sun rose. Apparently, news of the attempt on Mrs. King had spread. He started ignoring them as most were from news people, then Sanchez rang, and he picked up.

She didn't bother with a greeting. "What the hell are you doing, getting your ass shot?"

"Good morning to you, too. And it wasn't my ass, thank goodness. I'd never live that one down."

"How bad is it?"

"Just a scratch on my arm."

She swore in Spanish at him. Her familiar form of affection made him smile. His partner had refreshing ways of showing her concern. "Stop worrying. They just cleaned me up and bandaged it."

"This is why you need me."

"It's one of the many reasons I need you."

"You trying to butter me up?"

"Of course."

"Hadley told a few of the guys you should have caught him. Asshole."

"Just too many places for him to run on that part of the campus. He disappeared into the trees." But, damn it, for a change he agreed with Hadley. He should have caught him.

"That woman's lucky you get those weird hunches all the time. She would have been dead woman walking without them."

He sighed. "A sobering thought, that it all came

down to chance."

"When do you get your gun back?"

"The boss said he'll push it for this morning."

"Good."

Another call buzzed. "I need to run. Call you later."

"Bye."

The next call informed him the team who investigated the shootings and the IAB representative would see him at nine. *That works*. He had an endless list of things to do, so at least he could get one thing out of the way. The door creaked open, the sound grating on his ears, and he glanced up. Dayle stood framed in the doorway, dressed in her usual suit and blouse. She looked ready for another workday, other than the concern darkening her eyes. "Forgive my intrusion. I had to see for myself that you're all right."

Pleasure stole through him at the sight of her. Other than his partner, he hadn't had anyone who cared about him in a long time. "Come in."

She took a few steps inside, glancing around. "So, this is the mysterious lair of the dynamic Detective Black."

He chuckled. "Yes, when worn chairs and stained coffee cups come in fashion, we'll finally be in vogue."

She approached and touched him, letting her fingers trail over the bandage. "Just a scratch?"

"Yes. They always bleed like a pig, but it's just a little trough. Didn't even need stitches."

"Didn't need them or you just didn't bother?"

He shrugged. "I'm a good healer."

"Mrs. King has a lot to be grateful for."

"Actually, I was quite impressed with her. She

stayed really calm under the circumstances. Her husband was very appreciative, too."

"I would imagine he was. How did you figure it out?"

"Just dumb luck." He explained how he'd arrived at his conclusion and how he simply relied on instinct.

Her phone rang. She removed it from her pocket and answered. Replying in the affirmative a few times, she hung up. "Duty calls. I know you're going to be busy, but keep in touch, okay?"

"Will do." Elijah wanted to kiss her, but settled for walking her to the door instead. He smiled as he watched her exit, thinking that she looked just as good walking away as she did on her approach.

Better to keep his mind on his job for now. Time to head for his appointment.

Chapter Twelve

The killer called in sick to work, struggling to keep his voice at a relaxed pitch. That done, he stripped off his clothes, his shirt bloody from the shoulder wound. Holding his breath, he turned to look in the bedroom mirror. Just as he feared, his wound was an in and out. Somewhere in the woods around the university was a bullet covered in his DNA.

Damn that asshole! Where the hell had Black come from? Like a persistent bad smell, he just kept turning up where he wasn't wanted.

He'd had that uppity bitch in his sights, and his nemesis had seemed to materialize from nowhere. Had he given himself away? He ran through all the details in his head. *No.* It was impossible. If they knew it was him, they'd have been hammering at his door by now.

But how had Black anticipated the realtor might be next on his list?

Tired of all the annoying questions with no satisfactory answers, he stormed into the tiny bathroom, digging in a cluttered drawer to find some hydrogen peroxide and bandages. Cursing as he cleaned the wound, the liquid causing it to throb with pain, he finished by fixing cotton gauze on it with wide strips of adhesive tape. He had to stretch to treat everything on the back as well, causing every sinew to hurt even more.

That done, he stomped into the cramped den and turned on the television, ignoring the pervasive smell of old coffee grounds. He slumped on the worn couch to watch all the drama on the flickering screen. The news provided film of the expansive university grounds with an earnest reporter hugging a microphone. Turning up the volume, he soon tired of hearing the word 'hero' when they referred to Black and turned it down again.

Black had nothing to offer he didn't have, except a habit of kissing up to his superiors.

Two dead women to his credit, but, now, two misses as well. He wasn't performing as well as he'd anticipated, and that fact caused anger to flare. If his current methods weren't working one hundred percent, maybe he had to change things up a little. He had to inflict more damage.

But, how?

Time to figure it out.

****

Elijah breezed through the shooting team interview and got his gun back. The required review after an incident was to guarantee that no cop turned cowboy with a disregard for protocol. He certainly didn't, but he understood the necessity for proper procedure.

As soon as he returned, the lieutenant's assistant called to warn him about a press briefing at one-thirty. He knew it would be chaos, so he spent some time figuring what he could tell the reporters and what he couldn't. Letting the wrong information slip could prove catastrophic to his case.

So far, the King family had done what he'd suggested and kept to themselves. He'd found a basket of baked treats left on his desk as a thank you. In general, they weren't allowed to accept gifts, but the captain looked the other way on homemade baked goods. Anything he didn't eat would be vacuumed up by Sanchez when she returned to work on Friday. To keep her happy, he texted her about getting his gun back and the press conference.

She replied:

—*Better you than me. Smile! I'll be watching.*—

He missed her company and couldn't wait until she returned. Thankfully, the doctor had waived her week of desk duty because she had healed so quickly.

On his way to the press briefing, he passed Dayle in the corridor. Since there was no one nearby, he winked at her. Her answering smile cheered him and gave him the dose of energy he needed to carry on with his job. An old hand at handling the media, he filed in behind his superiors and waited his turn at the podium. The crowd seemed noisier than usual and, when his turn came, he waited until they quieted. He saw Pamela waiting, front and center, and let her ask her question first.

"Is this attack at the university last night connected to the previous murders of two professional women?"

He'd gone back and forth on this one, trying to decide how much to reveal, but came up with a middle ground. "We are looking into that possibility."

He chose another man with one of the major networks. "Does this attack have anything to do with the fact that Mrs. King is black?"

"At this point, the attack doesn't appear to be racially motivated, but we can't rule it out."

"So, it could be a hate crime?"

"It's possible."

The questions kept coming. "How did you happen to be at the university? Was it a coincidence?"

"I can't comment on that at this time."

"Do you have any further evidence on the previous murders?"

He and his bosses had agreed on his response to this one. "We have several promising new leads we will be investigating with all due haste."

And, a rather odd one that made a good closing point. "How much sleep did you get last night, Detective Black?"

He smiled. "Three and a half hours. It was a better night than some. That's all for today."

As usual, Elijah heard more questions echoing behind him as he left which he ignored. The glaring stage lights made him sweat, so it was refreshing to get out in the open hallway and duck out through a side exit. Without warning, Pamela Clayton appeared from around the corner, determination showing in the set of her jaw. "I want an interview."

She must have hustled to beat him outside. "Sorry. Too busy, and I don't have anything to add to what I just gave everyone, anyway." Smiling, he started walking, but she kept pace beside him, her camera man trailing a few strides behind.

"You know I'm always fair to the department, unlike most of these hyenas."

"It's not a question of fair, and you know it. Telling you anything else would hinder the investigation."

She lowered her voice. "Are you dating anyone?"

"You know I never talk about my personal life."

"I'm asking for myself."

Well, this is awkward, he thought with a wince. There was no way around it. He paused to meet her gaze, knowing she deserved that respect. "Yes, I am seeing someone. I'm sorry."

She shrugged, but he could see the pain of rejection in her eyes. It bothered him. "I'm not really your type anyway, am I?" she murmured, her voice softening.

He struggled to find words that wouldn't hurt her or obligate him.

"Never mind. It doesn't matter." She forced a smile. "We're still friends though, right? Even if you won't give me an exclusive."

"Of course, we are." He thought of a way to make it up to her. "I'll even ask my lieutenant about an exclusive after the case is solved, but no promises."

The stress left her eyes. "Thanks, Elijah. You're a good person."

"You're welcome."

He waited until she walked in the other direction before he resumed walking. Leaning into a sudden breeze, he continued back to his office. He felt sorry for Pamela. For all her glamorous looks and success, she seemed lonely to him. Until recently, he could relate, but Dayle had given him some hope that the future might have more to offer in that respect.

A welcome bit of news awaited him on his return. The crime scene technicians had found a bullet in one of the trees at the university. It had been from his Glock nine pistol, something he was sure of because of the direction. The bullet had been found close to where the killer had been standing when Elijah shot. It provided one welcome clue to follow. At least they might get DNA and a blood type. They'd have to wait for test results, though. If only the results went through the always overwhelmed laboratory as fast as they did on television shows.

He dropped in to talk to his lieutenant, suggesting he should call and warn the five other women on the list to take extra care in the near future. They went back and forth on the advisability of doing that. They didn't want to panic anyone. In the end, though, they agreed they couldn't take the chance of not warning them. His lieutenant offered to do it himself, thinking the women might take it more seriously from him.

It marked one thing off his to-do list, and he was grateful for the generous offer.

****

The killer watched the flash of D.A. Stockard's long, tanned legs as she passed by without giving him more than a distracted glance. Too busy, always too busy to give a decent man a second look.

All the men, hell, even a few of the women, paid attention to this bitch, their eyes tracking from her tits to everything below. She just gave them that fake smile and moved on as if she didn't notice. This woman should be a damned secretary, not building cases to go show off in a courtroom. She'd probably got her job on her knees, granting sexual favors to men with more power than her. He pictured her doing that, at the same time wishing he was on the receiving end.

Maybe that should be the next evolution of his crimes. He needed to shake things up. Instead of just killing the stupid sluts, he could spend a few days punishing them for their selfish acts. Would they realize before he killed them that on their knees is where they belonged in the first place?

The idea brought a rush of sexual pleasure. His body stirred. He had some vacation time due and the perfect place to house an unexpected guest. Just thinking about it made him hard. Hours of aching pleasure to satisfy him and, ultimately, a far more personal death.

Maybe he'd been cheating himself using a gun and staying at a distance. He flexed his hands. Large and strong, they could tighten around a woman's neck without any problem. Huffing in an excited breath, he smiled. He could take the next woman like that, and no one would even connect the crimes. A different location, a change in method and, presto, they'd never be connected. Black had enough other crimes to solve. He grinned, feeling on top of the world now.

Because who knew better how to stay one step ahead of the legal system than a cop?

****

Dayle stared at the glaring screen of the computer and sighed, rubbing her eyes. She thought it a miracle she didn't need eyeglasses yet, but she could tell the day was rapidly approaching. The paperwork proved endless in her line of work. When other people mentioned getting caught up on their workloads, jealousy swamped her. Try as she might, she never caught up on hers. The most reliable thing in the world was that, no matter what, people would always commit crimes.

There were so many pathetic excuses for taking away the rights of another. I had a lousy childhood, I needed or wanted it, and the most profound one—life's not fair.

Well, life isn't fair.

Get over it.

Others considered her a bit of a hard ass, but she'd been born with a practical nature. You had to work for what you wanted in life. No one achieved their dreams for free. She'd had a difficult childhood, but never used it as an excuse. Instead, she determined to prove everyone who doubted her abilities wrong, and she had accomplished her goal. You couldn't be a career woman in this world and not know what it was like to be slapped down, often by less talented or less hard-working people. She ignored them. Hard work and perseverance always paid off.

Her thoughts were disrupted by a sudden rap on her office door. She looked up to find Elijah standing there. "Hi. I thought you'd have gone home by now."

"I wish." He took a large paper bag out from where he'd been hiding it behind him. "Care for a bite?"

Her stomach growled, making them both laugh. "Sounds like you have excellent timing. I'd love one."

He moved over to sit in her cushioned guest chair opposite the desk. "You must be hungry. You didn't even ask what it is."

"When someone's kind enough to bring me dinner, I'm just not that picky."

His gaze met hers. "You didn't eat any lunch, did you?"

"No time."

"Now I know why you're slender. Let's see if we can make up for that." Opening the bags, he pulled out plates full of food carefully wrapped in plastic. "Chicken salad sandwiches with a side of fruit. The best brownies in the city for dessert. And you notice I just assumed you'd like company."

"Of course, I would." She looked up at him, absurdly touched, and stroked his arm. "You remembered my favorite sandwich."

He nodded. "I thought it might be a nice surprise at the end of a long day."

"There are no short days in our business, are there?"

"Not in my experience."

Setting the array of food on her desk, they peeled back the plastic and dug in with gusto. She almost moaned, the sandwich tasted so good with grapes and pecans that made her mouth come alive. "This is delicious."

"I'm glad you agree. The place where I bought it has been my favorite deli for years, and you know how proud New Yorkers are of their delis."

The chicken salad was, hands down, the best she'd ever eaten. The hearty multi-grain bread made her wish she had more time to bake. When she finished the sandwich, she found the berries and melon fresh and juicy. She sat back, sighing as she rubbed her stomach. "I'll have to save that huge brownie for later or I might explode."

"Have one tiny corner and tell me what you think."

She broke off a smidgen, taking a nibble and savoring the burst of flavor. "Oh, no, I'm sunk. I might live on these for the rest of my days."

He smiled. "I'm a brownie snob. It took me years to find the place that makes them just the way I like them."

"You really did make a very tiring day so much better." She tried, and failed, to remember anyone being so thoughtful in the past. "Thanks for that."

"I aim to please." He looked around. "Are you packing up for the night?"

"I think so. I'm beat."

"Well, get your things together, and I'll walk you to a cab."

She shoved a few thick files in her briefcase and grabbed her coat. He helped her slide it on and stood to one side until she locked her door. They chatted about their days' work as they rode the elevator down. Out in the street, he waved a cab over, and she smiled as he opened the door. "Goodnight, Elijah. Thanks for dinner." Reaching up, she kissed him, catching him by surprise before ducking to sit inside.

She read attraction and pleasure in his eyes before they drove away.

*****

The Rhymester watched his target kiss Black right on the mouth. The idiot stood on the curb and watched her drive away, his undeniable yearning easy to spot in his body language. When the hell had this relationship started? He hadn't heard anything about it, and gossip usually roared through the precinct like a fart in a tornado. After getting cranky about it, he realized something. His plan would double his fun, wouldn't it? If he managed to pull off kidnapping Stockard, he could sample the delicious D.A. at his leisure and stick it to Black at the same time. A glorious win/win situation for him, one that would catch the interest of newscasters everywhere.

At least the idiot's taste was improving. The last time he'd had the hots for a serial killer, for God's sake. And this was the guy the commissioner thought was so smart. He wouldn't think so at the end of this fiasco, would he? Just the thought of the end result made him grin. Another dead bitch and the destruction of super cop.

The potential scenario made Stockard so much more attractive to him. Snatching her would be a way to get headlines and screw with Black's head forever. He wouldn't be getting many headlines when it was revealed that he couldn't even protect his own girlfriend.

The idea settled in the recesses of his mind. He had another woman to take care of first to give him some relief from his building need.

And they would never see it coming.

Chapter Thirteen

On Saturday morning at the shelter, Elijah and Dayle helped the other volunteers stir the gallons of paint they'd purchased at the local hardware store. Afterwards, she passed out the brushes. The owner had agreed to give them fifteen percent off the cost of the supplies because it was for a charity. This morning, they would knock off the sleeping quarters which looked the dingiest and most depressing. The families had gathered in the play room to watch television so they wouldn't be underfoot. Elijah hoped for a few uninterrupted hours to get this chore done, then he would head back to work. His partner had returned yesterday to both cheers and ribbing about taking extra time off.

Ray and Sanchez had already started working on the far wall, laughing together as they spread a mellow blue over the drab gray. To Elijah's surprise, Seth Parker had shown up and was currently carrying a paint can and roller to the opposite side. Sara had welcomed them and laid out a big urn of coffee and some baked goods on a table off to the side as far away from the paint fumes as possible. She sucked in a breath of surprise. "I can't believe how much a little color cheers up the place."

There was a murmur of agreement. When a few more people showed up to help, Elijah took a break and led Seth to look at the kitchen. "You said you were a decent carpenter, right?"

"Yes. My father made his own line of furniture, and he taught me when I got old enough to wield the necessary tools."

He explained their plans for a large wooden table and storage. Seth peered at the space. "Just a thought, but you could make the seating against the wall built-in. That way, you could have even more storage underneath."

"Great idea. Do you think you could design something?"

"Sure. I'll work on it tomorrow." He turned to grin at Elijah. "So, you and Dayle are seeing each other?"

He nodded. "It's new, though. We're keeping it quiet."

"No worries. I won't add to the gossip mill. You're a lucky guy. Nice women who look that good are hard to find."

"Believe me, I feel lucky." Elijah's phone buzzed—an urgent call to a new crime scene. "Damn it."

"Need to go?"

"Yes. Sanchez, too."

"No worries. I'll keep an eye on things. We've got enough people here to get the room finished in no time."

"Thanks, Seth. I really appreciate it."

They made their way back to where the others were working. Dayle walked over to stand beside him, letting her hand rest on his arm. "Did you get a call?"

"Afraid so. Will you be okay here with Seth and the others?"

"Sure. We'll just keep busy with this. There's enough helpers now we'll get it done." She kissed his cheek. "Be careful."

"Okay, thanks. I'll call you later."

The crime scene was a picturesque mid-city park, a ten-minute drive away. Beautiful trees, every shade of green and gold, framed a less-welcoming spectacle. A crowd of onlookers had gathered, their cellphones raised to capture any possible gore. The sight of them turned his stomach. Whatever happened to compassion? Two patrolmen attempted to push the group farther away while waving the partners' car through the barricade.

Detective Hadley met them as soon as they exited the car, his usual sulky expression in place. "Thought you weren't going to make it," he said, glancing at his watch as if to make a point. "The lieutenant asked me to hold the scene until you arrived."

Elijah ignored the inference they were late. "What have we got?"

"Another gift from your guy. This one is posed for public display."

They ducked under the crime scene tape and followed him for thirty feet. A slender white woman, probably in her thirties, sprawled against the mottled bark of a stout oak tree. High branches towered overhead, casting eerie shadows across her face. A twisted rope around her slender chest anchored her in place. Her legs had been spread in a further degradation, revealing the bloody wound between them. The matching holes in her chest created a sickening, but familiar triangle. "We found identification in her pocket. Her name is Penny Appleby. Thirty-seven, single, runs here every morning, according to the woman who found her. Home address is located about three miles away from the park."

"Did the two women know each other?"

"No, apparently she just recognized her as a regular because they run at the same time." He shook his head. "Kind of a dumbass thing to do, be that predictable."

"Way to blame the victim, Hadley." Sanchez snapped on gloves and handed a pair to Elijah.

Hadley, of course, took offense at her words. "Oh, come on, I'm the bad guy here? Dude's probably been watching her for weeks and she's got earbuds on, drowning out the sounds that might have warned her."

Ignoring him, they took a closer look. The three bullets had left only a small amount of blood. Her heart hadn't kept beating long enough to provide more. "Anybody hear or see anything?"

He grunted. "Some of the rotten bastards took off before we could stop them. The few people who stayed only heard the other woman's scream when she found the body."

The crime scene technicians arrived and began their work, making way for Dr. Stafford to come bustling through, his worn, black leather bag in hand. A frown marred his expression. Settling in next to the body, he muttered, "This is getting old, Black."

The doctor deserved empathy. He had bodies piling up in the morgue that needed his attention, but this case had been flagged as their first priority. "We're making some headway, Doc. Maybe, this time, we'll get something more. He keeps tweaking his M.O."

A sigh was the medical examiner's only response. He inserted the liver probe and withdrew it to read the body's temperature. "She's only been dead about an hour, maybe ninety minutes. That's cutting it thin." Straightening, he added, "Getting a little cocky now, isn't he?"

He nodded. "As you know, arrogant killers make mistakes. That will work in our favor."

They pulled back out of the way so crime scene could finish with the corpse, then the doctor waved in the morgue attendants to remove it. He motioned Elijah to one side. "I'll do the autopsy right away. I heard rumblings the FBI may be brought in soon if we can't get a hold on this case."

"Yes. This third homicide will make it hard to deter them." He wanted to solve it with Sanchez, but knew they were running out of time. "I'll get this wrapped up as soon as I can and catch up to you at the morgue."

He and Sanchez searched all around the crime scene, looking for possible cameras on nearby businesses. No such luck. The killer had chosen his site well. It was far away from any buildings and shielded from the rest of the park by trees. Checking with the other cops, they found no one had received additional help from the onlookers.

Bear Davis volunteered to take Hadley in order to go and notify her next of kin. Elijah was pathetically grateful for two reasons: that he didn't have to do it, and it got Hadley out of the way. He knew from experience Hadley would leave the hard work to Davis who would do it as a matter of course.

He and Sanchez eventually made their way to the morgue. When they arrived, they found Dr. Hayes getting changed into a fresh cotton gown, the tie strings dangling down. Elijah turned to Sanchez. "Why don't you head up to the office and see what background information we can unearth on the victim? Find out if she's had some media exposure lately."

"That works for me." With a half-hearted wave to the others, she left. The morgue was her least favorite place, and he knew it. For him, the doctor's work always proved to be quite fascinating. The man was fastidious, often catching things that would have snuck past a less-talented person. Slipping on protective gear, he followed the doctor into the autopsy room.

Dr. Hayes murmured into the recorder, dictating date, time, and everyone's name. First was the external examination, checking skin, finger, and toenails for any evidence. Elijah heard an intake of breath and watched as he picked up a pair of small forceps and leaned forward. He gently parted the woman's lips and plucked something off them. "Well, well. Looks like we have a hair that's not hers." He looked at it under the magnifier. "Short and brunet."

"Maybe he stood over her afterwards." A surge of excitement gave him hope.

"Could be."

"She has a couple of odd contusions under her chest. See? Right here." Pointing to the side of her ribs, he thought about it for a moment. "Could he have shoved her as she ran past him? Pushed her down, then pulled his gun?"

"Possibly. It would have had to be on the grass, though, or she would have had more injuries to her legs from the pavement." He shook his head. "I'm afraid not having situational awareness in public contributed to this poor woman's death. It's not uncommon."

"He shoves her down, shoots her, then stands over her to gloat for a moment."

"Very likely. If you look at the stippling, you can tell these shots are from two to three feet away. She may have rolled on her back to confront him face to face." He shook his head. "Maybe he wanted to see her die close up. Isn't that a cheery thought?"

It wasn't, but, in all likelihood, his theory was correct. He stayed silent as the other man did a Y incision and, cracking the ribs, gained entry to her abdomen. Weighing the organs always seemed surreal to him. "Her organs are in excellent shape. She took her health very seriously." He took a step back. "Well, at least we got that single hair and a little more insight. Hopefully, that helps."

"Every clue helps. Maybe I can go back to the park witnesses and see if anyone noticed a tall, stocky brunet man who wasn't a regular. You never know." He stepped away. "Thanks, Doc. Hopefully you enjoy the rest of your weekend." He walked to the trash can, stripped off his gown, and left.

Walking back to the precinct, he checked his messages. Both Seth and Dayle had texted him that they'd finished painting the sleep room, cleaned up, and headed home. He sent them his thanks. Up in their office, he found Sanchez kicked back in his chair, peeling an orange. The unusual occurrence made him stare. "Since when do you eat fruit?"

"I promised Ray that for every three chocolate bars, I eat one healthy thing." She shook her head. "Gheesh, what a pain. You can't slip an orange in your pocket." He chuckled, knowing Ray would have an uphill battle against her proclivity for junk food.

"Gotta admit, though, they don't taste half bad." She offered him a section, and he ate it, the fragrant juice quenching his thirst.

"What did you find out about our victim?"

"Owns a string of yoga studios. Very popular, runs both group classes and privates."

"Any recent news articles?"

"An online magazine that specializes in health issues did a big spread about her and her studio three weeks ago."

He deserved a smack on the head. "Dammit. I didn't even consider online media."

"That's 'cause you're not into that kind of thing. Want me to scout around and see what other women have been profiled lately?"

"Won't that be a huge number?"

She shook her head. "Not if we stick to local women and the major sources. Which would make sense, right? As far as we know, this guy doesn't hunt outside the city."

"Yes, that makes sense. You do that. I'll call those witnesses back and see if anyone saw a tall, stocky, brunet man in the park before the attack."

"Where did ya get brunet?"

He explained about the hair they'd found. "And I could tell he was tall and stocky at the university."

"We're getting closer." She rubbed her hands together and got down to work. Cursing, she looked up again. "I meant to tell you Davis called. I guess when he and Hadley went to notify Appleby's parents, they basically said she'd taken a bad path anyway. They thought mom and dad meant drugs, but, no, that was a reference to her sexuality. She was a lesbian." She groaned. "What's wrong with people?"

"I agree. It's a shame. Easier to judge than to try and be more accepting, I guess."

A little depressed by the story, he got back to work. The first witness answered the phone, but, for the other two, he had to leave a message. He started a list of what they knew about their killer: male, tall, stocky, brunet, adept with knife and guns. Likely in his thirties because of the sophisticated nature of the crimes. A younger man wouldn't have the necessary control, an older man wouldn't be fit enough to escape with any speed. He realized he was assuming the attack on Sanchez and Clayton was connected, but he would follow his gut on that premise. Better to assume they were connected than ignore it and have regrets.

His lieutenant called in for an update, and he filled him in. "Let me know if you need more help. We're finally making some real progress. Let's get him."

"Yes, sir."

After he hung up, Sanchez said, "I found four more possible women to add to your list so far." She gave him the names. He made a note to call them later and advise them to take extra care. "There's something else you should know."

"What's that?"

"One of the local websites is promoting an in-depth interview with your girlfriend for next week."

The word girlfriend distracted him for a moment, then it clicked in. "You mean Dayle?"

Chuckling, she said, "You got a stack of other women lined up I don't know about?"

"She didn't mention anything about an interview."

"It's probably a common thing in her line of work.

No big deal."

It bothered him. Taking chances right now wasn't a good idea, not with a deranged killer on the loose. "I'll tell her to postpone it."

"You'd better ask her to postpone it unless you want to get your head slapped."

"You know what I mean."

"Didya ever think we could use that interview to set a trap? It could put an end to this once and for all."

Just the thought of using her turned his stomach to acid. Putting the two of them at risk was one thing, to involve a citizen was something else. "Hell, no. That's not something Dayle needs to get wrapped up in."

"What doesn't Dayle need to be wrapped up in?" When he looked up at the sound of her voice, he found the subject of his thoughts standing in the open doorway. She had to-go bags from the deli in her hands. "Thought you two might like a bite to eat."

"I might have to kiss you myself," Sanchez said, popping up to take one of the bags. "Thanks."

Dayle smiled and moved toward him with the other one. "They're both roast beef. I hope that's okay."

Since his partner was already digging in, that provided an answer on its own. "It's perfect. How about you?"

"I ate mine while they were preparing the other two." She leaned over to kiss his cheek, then settled on the edge of his desk. "Now, what big plan did I interrupt?"

He gave her some background on what they had discovered about the media articles being a link between victims. "Sanchez tells me you are being interviewed about your job next week."

"Oh, yes. I'd almost forgotten. It's an online piece."

"Any chance you can delay it?"

She shook her head. "I'm afraid not. It's been on the books for weeks, and the boss has been nagging me about raising my professional profile."

"It stays within this room, you understand, but we think that's how this killer chooses his victims. They all had some kind of interview before their murders."

"Oh, really?" Her gaze met his partner's. "We could look on this as an opportunity, you know. Couldn't we use it to lure him out?"

"That's what I said," Sanchez, said, looking smug. "That's what we were talkin' about when you came in. I told you she'd agree."

"Absolutely not," he said. "I'm not using either of you two as bait. We'll find another way."

His partner snorted her derision. "I know your protector gene is always in overdrive, but we're better equipped than most to make it work. Right, Dayle?"

"Right." She chose a softer approach to try and convince him. "We could set it up somewhere I was well-protected. I could wear a vest." She smiled. "I also know how to shoot, and I can always carry mace."

"I'd rather have the case handed to the FBI than risk your safety." He stayed silent as he finished the rest of his sandwich. He'd never experienced such a helpless feeling as when Sanchez got injured. Having Dayle in that position would be at least as bad if not worse.

****

The Rhymester sat, smiling, as he devised another rhythmic masterpiece for the paper. It made him laugh to send a poem about one victim to a woman who had almost been another victim.

At first, it had annoyed him when he found out this latest chick had been a lesbian. The body had barely been removed from the park before the rainbow brigade had shown up with flowers and tears. Second thoughts, however, made him rethink things. It would confuse Black and Sanchez which was always a good thing. He was an equal opportunity killer, obviously. Bitches were bitches, no matter who they screwed.

After working a good part of the afternoon, he finished it. Maybe by the time he was done, he'd have enough of these things to publish a book. What would he title it, he wondered. Maybe Poems from A Predator. Or better yet, Sonnets from a Serial Killer.

The possibilities were endless.

Chapter Fourteen

Elijah's day started with another quick call from Pamela and another poem.

Penny Appleby
A woman who runs alone in the park
Might run into madness hidden in the dark
Through her small ear pieces, music did play
Quite the laugh—I didn't even know she was gay
The Rhymester

Elijah sighed. At this point, he might never enjoy reading poetry again. This deviant was having way too much fun as he destroyed the lives of his innocent victims and their families. He was pathetically grateful that Sanchez had agreed to speak to the staff and clients at their victim's yoga studio. Fatigue and frustration were setting in, and he was running out of time. The only reason that the FBI hadn't been called in yet was that they were over-extended at the moment. It bought him and Sanchez a little more time to try and solve this case. Three murders and two foiled attempts had given them a sound, basic description and some DNA. What were they missing that could break the case wide open?

When Elijah couldn't work any longer, he dragged himself to his feet, grabbed his jacket, and headed downstairs. To his shock, he found Dayle waiting by the sergeant's desk, working on her laptop. Standing, she tucked her things away. She took his arm, said goodnight to the others, and exited with him.

"I'm so exhausted, I thought I was seeing things. I can't believe you waited for me." A hum of pleasure revived him.

She smiled. "Have you got the car tonight?"

"Yes. Ray picked Sanchez up."

"I thought I could tuck you in." She paused to smile up at him. "After that, I'll go home if that's what you want."

He ran his fingers down her arm and squeezed her hand. "My preference would be that you stay."

"Well, good. That would be my preference as well."

He thought for a moment about how special he had wanted their first night together to be, then shoved his concerns aside. Real life had a way of wrecking the best laid plans anyway. Whatever happened, there would be the pleasure of mutual discovery. When they reached the car, he saw her inside, then took his own seat behind the wheel.

The drive home was blessedly short. He ignored the telling thrum of his heart as it beat faster in anticipation. As soon as they stepped inside the entrance and he locked the door, she moved closer. Her arms looped around his waist, and she reached up, her lips warm and welcoming. Touching her felt different this time. Something vital between them had changed. Her body beckoned to his. He could feel her curves against him, and she fit in every way that counted. The knowledge that she had made the first move toward this ignited him in an unfamiliar way.

"Come upstairs," he murmured. He gestured her ahead of him as they climbed the staircase to his bedroom. Struggling to remain a gentleman, he couldn't help but notice the gentle sway of her hips. They entered and paused beside the bed. "I need a shower," he said. Meeting her gaze to make sure she was onboard with his intentions, he unbuttoned his shirt. She joined him without a word, mimicking his actions with her own clothing. A tremor worked through his body as her body was revealed to him one tempting piece at a time. "You're even more beautiful than I imagined," he said, moving toward her. "I've thought about this since we first spoke."

She reached a hand to touch his chest, her soft fingers sending a trail of electricity over his body. "Making the first move is much easier than I expected."

He led her into the bathroom by the hand, grateful for the larger shower he'd installed two years ago. Turning on the water to warm, he set two bath sheets on the corner, and they went inside.

Warm water streamed over them as he chose a fresh bar of soap and lathered her. He couldn't look away from her dark, expressive eyes. In their glimmering depths, he saw her answering desire, and a thrill traveled down his back. Her skin, so soft under his touch, reminded him of silk.

"Turn around." She took the soap from his hand and did the same for him. Her touch made him ache for so much more, and he schooled himself to patience. Her gentle fingers moved from his chest to his legs, exploring everything in between. After a while, it taunted too much, and they rinsed. Stepping onto the cushioned mat, he toweled her hair, then wrapped the fluffy bath sheet around her. She did the same for him.

Taking her by the hand, he led her to his bed. Any

sense of fatigue had long fled. As they dropped their towels, she lay down and slid over, making room for him. Struck by the surreal picture of her lying there, waiting for him, he joined her. The shock of her skin against his imprinted on his memory to savor later. Cupping her head to stare into her eyes, he said, "Tell me if I do anything you don't like. I want this to be all about your pleasure."

She smiled. "How about yours?"

"It's pleasure enough that you're here with me." He kissed her, then, as her mouth opened to him. Heat mixed with the simple acceptance of desire. Her hands began to roam, coaxing him to a realm where discipline waned. "You feel wonderful."

"I wondered what this would be like."

"Did you?"

"Yes...and even the rampant edges of my imagination fell short of this." His fingers stroked her breasts, and he heard her make a hum of feminine approval in her throat. Wandering farther, his hands found damp heat waiting, and she arched toward him. He pulled her closer and, shifting, nestled between her thighs. Watching the hungry expression in her eyes encouraged him. She murmured his name, and he pushed inside her, taking his time as she enveloped him in beckoning heat and softness.

Setting a slow rhythm took all his restraint. Had he ever experienced such compelling pleasure? It was as if their bodies were created to complement each other. He held her hips in his hands, and they moved together. The silky skin of her thighs glided against his, and the sensation stole his breath. Before long, she began to moan and thrash. "Elijah..."

"Shhh. I've got you." He picked up his rhythm, leaning to press his lips to the pulse that throbbed in her slender throat. When she came, he held her tight, holding off until he could wait no longer. Joining her in release, he gazed into her eyes, and all his emotions fell into place.

Home. Being with her was like coming home.

When every shudder waned, he moved to lie next to her, panting. After a moment, he reached down to cover them both with the comforter. When he lay back, she shifted to lie against his chest. He stroked her hair. "I was so happy to see you waiting for me."

She chuckled. "That's pretty forward for me, but it seemed like the right decision."

"I feel compelled to agree."

Kissing him, she said, "Now, get some sleep. I know you have to go back in the morning." She stroked his arm and, before long, he did as she suggested.

The sound of the shower woke him as the morning sun crept into the sky. He had a confused moment, still not quite awake, until he remembered and smiled. Tempted to join her, he realized neither of them would be on time for work if he did. Instead, he waited to enjoy the sight of her as she stepped out a few minutes later.

The image of her as she stood, silhouetted against the white tiles, toweling off, made his body hum with pleasure. "I can't think of a nicer scene to wake up to."

She looked up, and a pleased smile crossed her face. "You were still sleeping, so I thought I'd go first."

The husky timbre of her voice made him regret his responsibilities. "I considered joining you, but then we would both be late."

She laughed. "That's true."

He swung his legs out of bed, stood, and stretched, arms reaching toward the ceiling. Meeting her in the doorway, he leaned down and kissed her, rubbing a dot of water from her jaw with one finger. "Have you got enough time for a bite of breakfast?"

Glancing at the clock, she frowned. "Better not. I might be clean, but I still have to go home and change."

"Give me fifteen minutes, and I'll drop you off."

"How about your breakfast?"

Turning the shower faucet back on, he swiveled around and grinned. "I'll raid Sanchez's desk. I can always count on her having something sinful in the desk drawer I can eat."

He was a man of his word. Fourteen minutes later, they exited the front door. As soon as he eased into traffic, she said, "You really are very punctual."

"I was late once because of a flat tire, and Sanchez panicked. I texted her eight minutes after I was due to arrive, and she'd already called the hospitals to check on accidents."

"That's hilarious." She paused. "I like her energy and her sense of humor. Ray's, too."

He nodded. "Yes. She chases him around, and he settles her down a bit. It's the perfect balance."

"That makes sense. You were married at one time, right?"

"Yes. For four years." He knew what was coming, but it didn't bother him.

"Do you mind me asking why you divorced?"

"No, I don't care. I'm afraid I have to take the majority of the blame for that failure. I'm pretty dedicated to my job, and Lynn said I didn't have enough time for her. She may have had a point."

"But you were a cop when you married her, right? She knew long hours were involved."

"Yes. I was fresh out of the academy and very eager to prove myself. I just think most spouses don't understand the sheer man hours required to make your mark in my line of work."

"Especially when you want to be a detective."

"Exactly."

"Do you ever see her?"

"No. She's remarried and lives in Connecticut, now. Three children, white picket fence, and the whole deal." He made his way through one light and slowed for the next. "How about your ex-husband? Does he live nearby?"

Her body stiffened. Looking away from him, she shook her head. "No. He lives in Los Angeles."

The tone of her voice alerted him that she'd rather avoid the subject. Not wanting to make her uncomfortable, he switched to asking about her plans for the day. Her shoulders relaxed. "Mostly case preparation today and one court case this afternoon that should be quick and easy."

"Plea bargain?"

"Yes."

"It would be nice if more cases could be handled that way. The court's backlog wouldn't be nearly as challenging." He swung up in front of her apartment building. "Well, don't work too late."

"I won't." She leaned to kiss his cheek. "Thanks for the drive and…everything else."

"It was very much my pleasure."

Flashing him a smile, she shut the door with a

muffled thump. He watched as a man held open the front door of the building, his gaze appreciative as she entered. Forcing his attention to work, Elijah headed for his garage.

His mind crept back to her as he climbed the stairs to his office. The one thing that had bothered him last night was a scar he'd seen on the side of her lower abdomen. Asking about it would have upset her, but his curiosity wouldn't let it go. He'd seen a lot of injuries in his career, and he recognized a knife scar when he saw it. There was a story there. He hoped that, someday, in the near future, she would trust him enough to tell him about its history.

****

Elijah received a text from Seth as he sat at his desk drinking his morning coffee.

—I know you're busy, but I have plans drawn out for that kitchen unit for Homestead. Want me to email them to you?—

He'd need a lunch break anyway. Might as well kill two birds with one stone.

—Do you have time for a quick lunch today? I want to bounce an idea off you. You could bring the plans along.—

—Sure. Smithees at noon work for you?—

—Yes. See you then.—

Smithees was an old diner the local cops frequented, the spot convenient and familiar for both him and Seth. A retired detective owned the place, and he made the generous servings overload the confines of the plates. The interior was nothing to brag about, but the old guy could seriously cook and cheap food, hefty platefuls, and camaraderie kept the boys in blue coming through the door. Elijah wouldn't need any dinner after a meal there.

Working at his desk all morning didn't yield any significant progress. At 11:45, he walked Sanchez to the door, and they headed off in opposite directions. She would grab a quick lunch with Ray while he met Seth.

Not surprisingly, the restaurant was already half full when he arrived, old rock and roll playing in the background. Pausing by the door to take his coat off, he saw Seth raise a hand from the back to attract his attention. He made his way there, nodding to a few familiar faces on the way. Several people watched to see who he was meeting. Cops tended to be nosy. It came with the territory. "Hey, Seth," he greeted the other man, stretching out a hand to shake. He slid into the opposite side of the red vinyl booth and settled his forearms against the worn melamine table. "Thanks for meeting me."

He smiled. "Nice to break up the day with a friend. Want to order so we can talk and eat?"

"Sounds good." He looked at the battered vinyl menu and chose what he thought of as the least harmful option: a grilled chicken sandwich with extra vegetables and ice water. It amused him that Seth chose the same thing. He knew the other man worked out daily and probably watched his calories, too.

After the curvy waitress took the orders, giving Seth a teasing wink, she hurried back to the bustling kitchen. His friend pulled a piece of paper from an inside pocket, handing it to him across the table. "The plan's pretty basic, but I think the table and storage should work fine. I took the measurements after you left the other day."

Elijah looked it over, impressed with the scaled drawing, done on graph paper. "It looks perfect. Should we show it to Sara Towers before we order the lumber?"

"I already sent one to her to see if it would work. I hope that's okay. She was pretty enthusiastic, but I told her I wanted to show it to you first."

"Oh, that's fine. Can you order the lumber and other supplies we need, and I'll reimburse you for it?"

"Sure. I'll call the list in later today. Any chance you can give me a hand for an hour or two on the weekend? I'll custom cut everything, so it should be easy to put it together on site."

"I can take a few hours Saturday morning, barring emergencies."

He grinned. "Maybe Dayle can give us a hand."

"I'll be sure to ask her."

"How's that going?" he asked.

"Suspiciously well which makes me a little paranoid. Until her, my track record was a little shaky."

"I know what you mean. This business is hell on a relationship. It isn't for everyone."

"Are you seeing anyone?"

Shaking his head, he said, "Haven't been too interested in anyone, lately." He took a drink of his water. "This city's hard on us single folks, and I'm not interested in dating apps. Been there, done that, and it wasn't pretty."

They paused while their waitress delivered their sandwiches. The thick slabs of homemade bread held fresh vegetables along with a thick slab of seasoned chicken. The aroma of rosemary drifted up. Nodding their thanks, they dug in. After a few bites, Elijah paused. "I wanted to ask you if you've ever thought of taking the detective's exam."

Seth tilted his head, looking amused as he finished his bite. "What, are you a mind reader or something?"

"What do you mean?"

He shrugged. "I enjoyed working with you on the Marks' scene, and I've been toying with the idea ever since."

"Good. I think you should. You're very detail-oriented and observant, probably the two most important things. Plus, you get along well with others."

He met his gaze. "I don't get along with Hadley, but he's the rare exception."

Elijah laughed. "Nobody gets along with Hadley except Davis who's cornered the market on patience. Don't worry about it."

"I heard the exam's pretty tough."

"Do you like to read?"

"Yes."

"Then as long as you study, you'll be fine. It's a lot of memorization and simple common sense. Usually, the people who struggle are the ones who don't like to read in the first place." He smiled. "The hours are lousy, but it's a little more money, more respect, and definitely more interesting. You've done your share of years on the beat. There's an exam coming up in two months. Start right now, take it seriously, and you'll be fine."

Nodding, he took a bite of his sandwich, chewed, and swallowed. "Speaking of Hadley and other assorted assholes, did you hear what happened at Mike's bar the other night?"

"No. We've been pretty tied up with this case."

"I guess Hadley got pretty hot under the collar with some woman he was interested in, and Davis had to intervene."

It caught his attention, maybe because nothing the jerk did surprised him. "That's the first time I've heard of him causing trouble outside the precinct."

Seth nodded. "Me, too. I guess he asked her out and when she refused, he just kept repeating 'Why not? Give me one good reason.' " He shook his head. "She just kept backing up, and he followed her toe-to-toe. He should be glad Davis was around to talk some sense into him. That's some serious shit."

"Did Davis persuade him to leave the bar?"

"Yeah. I guess he even insisted on driving him home to make sure he sobered up."

"He'd better hope the lieutenant doesn't hear about it."

"I know. He's not the brightest bulb in the pack."

They polished off their sandwiches. Afterwards, Seth sat back with a sigh. "As far as the detective exam goes, I appreciate your support, Elijah. I think I'm going to do it. At this point in my life, I think I'm ready for a change."

"Absolutely. And if you need some help studying, let me know. Be glad to help." He picked up the tab for lunch over Seth's protests. "You can get it next time."

"Fair enough." They ventured out to the street together and parted ways at the door. Walking back to the precinct, Elijah reflected on the fact that it satisfied him to help someone move forward as he had. The department needed more Seth Parkers and fewer Hadleys. Whining and taking the easy way out didn't get the job done, but hard work always did.

****

Dayle tried to keep her mind on her towering pile of paperwork, but the memory of last night's encounter with Elijah kept distracting her. Who knew that a reserved man like him would make such a wonderful lover?

Quite a daring move, waiting for him like that, but she'd been a coward for too long. Her confidence in dealing with men had been shattered for years, but, somehow, he made her feel more adventurous. The intensity he'd brought to the bedroom surprised her and appealed to her hidden romantic streak. Sexual pleasure had played hide and seek with her libido until now. He'd made her needs a priority, and her release had been unparalleled. If she looked in the mirror, she was sure her smile would reveal secrets better kept to herself.

He'd been painfully honest about his part in his unsuccessful marriage, and she appreciated his honesty. Sometime soon, she would tell him about her disastrous marriage. If there was a contest about who'd made the worst choice, she'd win, hands down. She hadn't wanted to spoil the morning after by delving into that thorny subject.

She knew he'd seen the scar, had in fact pressed his lips against it as if to soothe her. It brought a tear to her eye that he'd chased away with pleasure. The fact that he never pushed her about anything made him such easy company. For the first time in many years, her private life encouraged thoughts of the future. But, for now, she'd better get back to work or she wouldn't have a job.

****

Sanchez returned from interviewing the young staff at the yoga studio around eleven.

"Find out anything useful?" Elijah leaned against the chair, stretching his back.

"Nah. She was a great boss, it's a tragedy, blah, blah, blah. Lots of tears and red faces." She hopped on the edge of the desk. "She and her manager were close friends, and the woman said she kept her sexuality more or less a secret." She shook her head. "Remember the demonstrators in the park? I guess more people had figured it out than she thought."

"How close were she and the manager?"

"They weren't lovers. She's married to a dude. I guess the victim's parents are super religious and she didn't want them to know. That's the reason for all that talk about taking the wrong path."

He thought it through. "I bet the killer didn't know. Or maybe he just didn't care about her sexual orientation. What do you think?"

"He hasn't raped any of them. Maybe their sexuality doesn't matter to him."

"Is he wandering off script or just getting sloppy about his research? Or, like you said, is it a case of any woman will do?"

"I dunno." She lifted an eyebrow. "You look awful chipper today."

He smothered a smile. "Finally got some sleep for a change."

She peered into his face, squinting. "I don't know, friend. You still got shadows under your eyes, but you're smilin' ear to ear. Anybody keeping you company under the bedcovers?"

A telltale heat came to his cheeks, and he tried to will it away.

"You dog, you."

"I didn't say anything," he protested. "You have a great imagination."

She pointed a finger at him, close enough he could take a bite if he was so inclined. "I know that look. That's a quiet guy's way of saying, 'Hell, yes.' " She slapped him on the arm. "Good going."

"Can we get back to the case now?"

"If we have to."

"See what else you can dig up on social media. I'm going to talk to the boss and see if we can track down a policewoman we could use to try and set a trap."

"Dayle offered."

"Too risky. But maybe we can find someone who looks enough like her to pass. Tall brunettes can't be that rare." Walking down the hall, he rapped on the door frame and his lieutenant looked up. "Do you have a few minutes for an update?"

His boss put down the paper he'd been reading. "Sure. Take a seat."

He ran through the facts on the latest victim and the leads they were pursuing. After getting him up to date, he mentioned their idea of a trap. "Stockard offered to do it, but she's next best thing to a civilian. It's too risky. But what if we had her include a few taunts in the interview to goad him? Then, when it comes to setting the trap, we substitute a police woman in her place, somewhere we can control."

"Not a bad idea. Have you got anyone in mind?"

"No, but there's bound to be someone close enough in looks. He won't get near enough to see the imposter in time."

He nodded, looking thoughtful. "I think the idea has some merit. Go ahead and come up with a game plan. If we don't think out of the box, I don't think we'll catch him."

"Yes, sir."

****

Early this morning, Detective Jones had watched Dayle Stockard kiss Black on the cheek before he dropped her off. His alter ego, The Rhymester, might even be tempted to write a sonnet about it. Isn't that sweet, he thought as she walked away. Black had obviously bedded her, but he couldn't believe that the lieutenant's pet could satisfy a woman like her. *Give me a chance.* He would make her scream in every way she could imagine and a few she couldn't.

Stockard was tall and fit, but if she expected to win against a man in a fight, she was in for a surprise. The most difficult part would be exactly how to gain access to her. She worked long hours, and her office was well-protected. Her hobbies were a mystery. She didn't blab the way so many of the dumb bitches did, and she had non-existent social media going on.

It would be his biggest challenge yet. One with a newly imagined reward before death.

She would be the first one he'd rape before he killed her, the first one he'd take in private rather than in public. Hell, he could put in for some time off and hold her for days. What was better than one rape? Ten or twelve. The possibilities were endless.

When he was done with her, she'd never give him that blank smile and walk past him again.

Chapter Fifteen

The thorough staff search took most of the afternoon, but he and Sanchez finally found a detective in another precinct who was a close enough match to Dayle. Her height and hair were very similar. From a distance, those would be the most distinguishing features. Their lieutenant made a call to her boss. He was willing to loan her for their sting when plans were solidified.

After a lot of discussion, they decided the most believable plan might be to stage a dinner out with Elijah, then have him called away, leaving her to find her way home. They scoped out a lot of possible restaurants before deciding on one which had a darker entrance with a few nearby alleys where bad guys could lie in wait.

The next afternoon was the day before the interview. Dayle joined them for an hour so they could discuss burying a few taunts to the killer in the information she provided. The three of them sat, sipping coffee, in their office. Elijah spoke first. "Are you comfortable with people knowing we're dating?"

"Of course, as long as it serves a purpose and isn't just for gossip."

"The reason I ask is that you could stress the equality of such a relationship. You don't even have to say my name, just that you're dating a detective. He understands you are equal partners, and he's happy to cook your dinner if you work late."

"You're a terrible cook. You told me so yourself."

"But I'll buy you dinner if you work late." He grinned. "The point is, that's the kind of thing that's going to push his buttons. Having a man in the kitchen instead of a woman."

"Good idea. And how about mentioning that we had to come to terms about salary because the D.A.'s office pays better than the police department."

"Ouch." He gave a mock wince. "No, that's perfect." He got serious, meeting her gaze. "After this interview, you'll have to take extra care, especially traveling back and forth to work. We should wait a few days after to allow him to make his plans. You need to keep a low profile just until it's done."

"Who did you get to be the fake me?"

"A detective from one of the other precincts. Her name is Susan Carmichael."

"Does she really look like me?"

"Same height and body type. Her hair is similar, too. We can enhance with makeup to alter her face a bit."

"Will she wear a microphone?"

"A mike and a tracker in case of emergencies."

"Sounds foolproof."

He shook his head. "Nothing is foolproof, but I think it should work."

"Okay." Sighing, she stood. "Better get back to paperwork, I guess. Let me know how my substitute makes out."

"Will do." Watching her leave with regret, he got back to work.

****

Around eight-thirty, he took a chance and walked to Dayle's office to see if she was still working. As the elevator doors opened, she walked out, smiling when she saw him. "I hope you're coming for me."

Security were the only people left that he could see, but he still lowered his voice as they moved to the door. "I was hoping we might catch up on some sleep together."

"That's the best invitation I've had all day."

"How about we might swing by your place to get you some fresh clothes, then go back to my place. Is that okay?"

"That's lovely." She took his hand as they walked to the car. "You look stiff. Are you okay?"

"I'm fine. Just a few too many hours slumped over a desk, I guess."

She smiled up at him. "I've heard a back massage can do wonders for things like that."

"Are you volunteering?"

"Absolutely."

"I'll gladly take you up on that." He opened the door for her, waiting as she slid inside and settled her briefcase on the floor. As they drove to her apartment, he told her about his lunch with Seth.

"It's nice of you to encourage him."

"We need more men and women like him. He knows how to work hard and pay attention. And he seems to have a good rapport with everyone he works with."

"He was thoughtful enough to help out at the shelter, too."

"Exactly."

Elijah went upstairs with her when they arrived at her place. For some reason, she didn't match her surroundings. Oh, they were very elegant, but lacked personality. He wandered into the bedroom, amused to see her bed was unmade. She noticed his glance and chided him. "Oh, I know. I never make mine until right after I get home in the evening. Even then, I just spread it up and immediately set out my clothes on the chair for the next day. Isn't that awful?"

"Actually, I do the same thing myself, so it amused me." He wandered into the attached bathroom as she grabbed a few cosmetics off the countertop to go with her. "Shower in the morning or at night?"

"Always morning. I'd never wake up otherwise." She poked her head out. "Mind you, I might add a night time one if I had company."

A jolt of heat ran through him, and he met her gaze. "Good to know."

Laughing, she zipped her case and opened her closet. She selected a suit and blouse. "Why don't you carry the case? I'll take this so I can lock the door and set the alarm."

After settling in the car, they made their way to his house, grateful the traffic was light. Letting them into the house, he closed and locked the door behind them. "Make yourself comfortable. I'll take these upstairs and make us something to eat."

Upstairs, he hung her clothes in his closet, surprised by the pleasure the small gesture caused. He set her case beside his dresser and turned to head back down, only to find her standing in the doorway. "Aren't you hungry?" he asked, allowing her to fit the meaning to her wish.

She laughed and took a few teasing steps toward him. "Sometimes, satisfying hunger starts with a backrub." Reaching up, she undid his tie, flinging it onto the nearby chair. He liked the playful light in her eyes and let her set the pace. She undid the buttons of his shirt, one by one, letting her fingers play against the hair of his chest. After tugging it out of the waistband, it joined the tie.

"Allow me," he said, barely touching her before she waggled a finger at him.

"You just wait and watch." She reached for his belt buckle, going slow enough for his patience to wear thin. After a moment, he was naked, and she still had her clothes on. "Lie down." Her husky tone took the sexual tension up another notch. He did as she asked, watching as she slipped her blouse off. She knew what she was doing to him. He could tell by the smug expression on her face.

At this very second, he was the luckiest man in the universe.

When her bra joined her blouse on the floor, his heart revved. The sound of the zipper on her skirt sounded like a taunting countdown. He wanted to grab her and throw her down on the bed. Only discipline kept him in place. She was the very definition of beauty to him with her long hair cascading down to her nipples. His own piece of art.

The mattress dipped as she knelt beside him on the bed. "Turn on your stomach."

Elijah was a very smart man. He did as he was told. As she mounted his hips, her body glided against his, and he almost groaned out loud. Then her hands began to rub, starting at his shoulders and working their way down. Her fingers dug into all the tight, bunched muscles, and now he did groan in pleasure. "Oh, that feels amazing."

She chuckled. "I've barely begun."

"You're going to kill me, but it's a worthy way to die," he murmured. After ten minutes of her treatment, his body turned into a bowl of jelly. She moved over his buttocks and down his legs, rubbing and pummeling. He was so relaxed, he might have slept except for one thing. Her touch had caused a predictable response. One part of him was most assuredly not relaxed.

"Turn over."

He did as she requested, meeting her beautiful eyes. With a satisfied smile, she swung her leg over him again. Easing up his body, she fit her legs around his hips and rubbed against him like a cat. He was so glad to feel her wet heat because he wasn't sure he could wait any longer. As if she knew, she raised up on her knees and took him inside her. He murmured her name, and she began to move, holding him tight by the simple grasp of her toned muscles.

Reaching up, he stroked her breasts. "Your skin feels like satin," he said, thrusting up to meet her. The glide of her thighs against him drove him mad.

She threw her head back, murmuring sounds of pleasure reaching him now. To him, she looked like a temptress who men could never ignore. Not this man at least. He picked up the tempo, driving into her, desperate to ensure her pleasure. When her body tightened, he touched where they were joined and she came with a loud moan, her body spasming around him. Content now, he let himself be beckoned into an almost endless orgasm. They held each other, gasping, until they were both replete.

Holding her tight, he shifted so that she lay beside him. He ran his hands through her hair, cupping her head. Their heartbeats finally slowed. Smiling, he said, "I'm not sure I've ever had such an amazing experience before."

"That was the goal," she whispered, touching his cheek.

"Goal met and surpassed."

They stayed wound around each other for a while, then empty stomachs had them dressing in comfortable clothes before digging in the refrigerator for leftovers. After that, they went back to bed and slept deeply, undisturbed, until morning.

In the morning, they had an extra-long shower together, then had to hurry to work, armed only with a trail mix bar each for breakfast. Neither of them missed a big breakfast. As he dropped her off at work, he kissed her. "Good luck with the interview. Let me know how it goes."

"I'll do my best. Talk to you later."

Full of unusual cheer, he started the day with a burst of energy.

****

Dayle had done plenty of interviews, both live and in print, but this one made her more conscious than any of them. Talking to the media was considered an essential part of her job, so she wasn't nervous per se. She just wanted to lay enticing bait for the murderer as Elijah and Sanchez had asked.

It didn't help that the young man, with the unlikely name of Ace McDonald, clearly believed he was God's gift to anyone of the female persuasion. The polar opposite of anyone who would catch her eye, he had gym rat muscles, a purchased tan, and slicked back blond hair. His gleaming, bleached teeth seemed to stretch his mouth so he looked like a shark. Trying to peer down her blouse seemed to be his favorite pastime which really annoyed her.

Use him. Sitting in the cramped booth where they recorded the segment, she struggled to stay focused on the ultimate goal of this interview. The first handful of questions were what she called fluff, but she managed to steer them in a more serious direction.

"Is it hard to keep a relationship going when your hours are so demanding?"

Bingo. He probably thought of this question as flirting, but she could use it for her own goals. "Actually, my boyfriend is a homicide cop, so he understands. Whoever makes it home first cooks dinner, and he's fine with that. We are partners. Our careers are equally important."

A petulant expression spread over his face. "Care to share his name? Everyone loves a little gossip."

"I'm afraid not. I try to keep the details of my private life out of the media's eye."

"Doesn't your work mean that sometimes you are on opposing teams?"

She smiled. "We are all on a team that seeks justice." Great. Now she sounded like a billboard promoting the legal system.

"Is it difficult for your significant other that your office pays significantly more than a cop makes?" The sneer on his face made her cranky.

At least she didn't even have to try to force that question. "Actually, he's very proud of me. It's not uncommon anymore for a woman to earn more than a man or for a man to stay home with growing children. That's what true partners do."

He followed with a number of boring questions that everyone asked. They wound down from there, and she hoped she'd done enough. Now that Ace had finally clued in to the fact that she wasn't interested in him, he barely said goodbye, hustling her out the door as soon as the segment wound down.

She texted Elijah to tell him she thought it had gone well.

****

Elijah read her text and smiled. In three days, they would set the trap and hope they caught him. Susan Carmichael was on board, and he'd picked a few other detectives he could count on to provide coverage. Hadley had apparently complained to Lieutenant Porter about not being included. When the boss asked why, Elijah had been quite honest with him about not wanting to rely on Hadley. He was always hesitant to be critical of another detective, but he didn't trust the other man to have his back.

They had finally got a return call from one of the witnesses from the park. He had been out of town on business, but called to say he had seen a man dressed in black who didn't look like they belonged among the others in exercise clothes. Although he wasn't sure he could tell him much more than tall and brown-haired, he agreed to work with a sketch artist to try and help. They set up an appointment for tomorrow morning.

On the job bright and early the next day, Elijah got the bad news first thing in the morning before Sanchez arrived. Dismayed, he listened to another detective report that Susan Carmichael had been injured in a car accident the previous night. A felon they were chasing had rammed her car with his own. Luckily, she had survived with some injuries, but they included a broken leg. Their sting for the next night was a no-go unless they could find a last-minute replacement.

"Damn it."

Sanchez hustled through the door, her arms full of a big box of donuts. "What's goin' on?"

He explained what had happened.

"But it's all set up for tomorrow night," Sanchez said, talking around a bite.

"It can't be helped. Her leg's in a cast."

"Is there another female detective or even a beat cop who would work?"

He shook his head. "I don't think so. The only other woman we found who was tall enough to pass is pregnant."

"Well…"

"No."

"You didn't even let me speak."

"You're thinking about using Dayle again. There's no way I'm going to put her at risk."

"She should make that decision, not you. It's not like she'll be by herself. We'll have protection in every corner."

He met her gaze. "We both know that things go wrong during these setups all the time, despite best intentions. People get hurt. It's not in her job description to act as bait."

He was interrupted by another call which seemed to take forever. Sanchez filled the time texting, her fingers a blur of motion. When he finally got off the line twenty minutes later, she continued to try and persuade him. Fed up, he put an end to it by standing. "I'd better update the lieutenant and get his take."

Reluctance had him dragging his feet. He knew that if he filled his boss in, the likelihood was that the FBI would be called in to take over. It couldn't be helped. When he turned the corner to rap on the door, he found Dayle sitting in his boss's office. Surprise, closely followed by suspicion, had him frowning. "I'm sorry. I didn't mean to interrupt. I'll come back later."

"No need." Porter waved him inside. "We were just talking about your case. I heard your decoy was injured."

"Yes, sir. We'll work on finding another policewoman, but it will take time."

He gestured him to the seat beside Dayle. "I think we have a reasonable solution, but I've been informed you're not happy with the idea."

It was true. That warning chill he'd had when he saw her there was legitimate. "Sir, using citizens in a sting has never worked well. It's too risky."

"Dayle isn't exactly a typical citizen, is she?"

"No, but—"

"I think this might be our only chance of catching him, Black. We are running out of time on this one. If we don't catch him, I'll have to call in the Feds, and none of us want that."

"I'd rather let them take over than allow her to get injured."

"She can wear a vest, carry a gun, and wear a tracker. You can hand pick the people you want to help you, however many you need." He sighed. "We have to stop him, one way or the other."

He looked back and forth between them. "Between you two and Sanchez, it appears I'm outnumbered."

"It'll be fine, Elijah." Dayle smiled. "And we can have a celebration and finally get some real sleep when it's done."

A few moments later, they left the office. He didn't speak until they were out of his boss's hearing. Trying to keep frustration at bay, he asked, "Did Sanchez tell you about Carmichael?"

Making no attempt to prevaricate, she answered, "Yes. She texted me. Don't be angry with her."

"She knew this wasn't what I wanted."

"Hey." She pulled him to into a quiet nook where they couldn't be overheard. "I love that you're a protective person, but I'm a tough cookie. I can take care of myself."

"So tough that you've been stabbed before?" The burst of words came out of nowhere. He wished at once he could take them back when he saw the shocked expression on her face. "I'm sorry, Dayle. I shouldn't have said that. It's just that taking unnecessary risks is not in my wheelhouse."

She huffed in a breath and let it trickle out. "Surviving that attack ultimately made me a more confident person. I escaped an abusive husband and learned that we can never let those men win. That's part of the reason I want to help, both here and at the shelter." She put a consoling hand on his arm. "Did you ever hear that saying about evil thriving if good men and women do nothing? This is a textbook case. We have to do something to put a stop to these murders."

He leaned down to put his forehead against hers. "Okay. I'll have to trust your instincts on this. But you have to promise me if anything goes south, you'll bail and save yourself."

"Deal." She glanced around, and seeing no one nearby, kissed his cheek. "When do we have the big meeting when we nail down the particulars?"

"Tomorrow at three. The dinner reservation is at seven. That will give everyone four hours to go over the details and finish preparations."

"Okay. Your office, three sharp. I'll see you then."

He watched her walk away, her confident stride making a mockery of his fear. This case gave him the twitches. He couldn't help but wonder what tiny sliver of information he was missing that could solve it.

When he arrived back at the office, he and Sanchez ran over the list of people who would take part. They took a drive to check out the exterior of the restaurant to ensure that nothing had changed. So far, so good. Security cameras were on every nearby building— they'd already checked to make sure they were functional.

Four of the men would be outside, two in front, two in back for better coverage. The two female cops would be inside, one bussing tables and one serving. Impossible to know if their killer would follow her outside or already be waiting. They would sit at the most visible table.

Around eight p.m., they parted company and headed home. When he arrived, he texted goodnight to Dayle and told her he missed her. She replied with a string of funny emojis in an obvious attempt to cheer him. At this point, he just wanted tomorrow to be over.

Chapter Sixteen

In an ironic twist of fate, they'd asked Jones to help with the sting. When he was well away from the precinct, he'd laughed so hard tears rolled down his face. He'd wanted to reply, "Too little, too late, losers."

So, they thought he was the perfect person to play a homeless bum on the street during their precious sting? He had a much more challenging part to play—the brilliant killer who carried off the hero's girl from right under their noses.

It was true that Dayle Stockyard didn't keep regular office hours. No one in the District Attorney's office did. Despite that, he always knew when she was leaving. She came in early and left late most nights. Her desk lamp, its light clearly visible from the front window, would click off and she'd magically appear at the entrance five minutes later.

Tonight was no different.

As he waited, he thought about that ridiculous social media interview meant to entice him. That would be a great plan if one of the other detectives hadn't already told him what was going on. But if it led her to relax her guard, all the better.

He knew Black had gone home around eight, but she worked an hour later than that. Finally, three minutes ago, her light had flicked off. Keeping his position in the shadows, he waited for the next sight of her. The flow of business people had thinned long ago. She always walked down from the building entrance about twenty feet to wait for her ride where it was less congested. Even though there weren't many pedestrians around tonight, habit was a powerful thing.

He stood in a convenient dark alley a mere five feet away from that spot, a taser clasped in his sweaty hand. Timing was everything. The glass doors swooshed open and she strode out, her high heels beating a subtle rhythm on the cement walk. Counting the steps as she walked toward him, he saw only two young women nearby. Their heads were bowed together, facing the opposite direction, their mouths blabbing nonsense as only the young can do.

She passed him. Lurching forward, he held the taser to Dayle's neck. Her body stuttered and spasmed. When she slumped, he put his arm around her waist and pulled her into the alley, out of sight. The whole thing took a mere five seconds. Once she stopped twitching, he lifted her and carried her swiftly to his older sedan parked at the other end of the alley. His heart pounded with excitement. He opened the back door and lay her on the seat, shoving her ankles away from the door. She was so damn tall, she took up every inch of the entire length of the space. Spreading the plastic tarp over her, he paused to squeeze her breast, a taste of what would come later. It all took less than three minutes before he started the car and put it into gear.

Adrenaline spiked, the pleasure orgasmic, as he eased out of the alley and into traffic. Intent on avoiding detection, he forced himself to obey the speed limits. Thinking about his preparations as he drove thrilled him. He'd opened up his stepfather's house a few days ago to air it out. The old place was in decrepit shape which was why it had sat on the market for so long with no buyers.

The second living area or parlor would make a wonderful home for his stylish new girlfriend. He'd boarded up the second entrance to it and reenforced the locks on the remaining one. His bastard of a stepfather had always said his construction skills were average at best, but he proved him wrong once again. Moving a bed inside for him and Dayle to share had been exciting. Sturdy leather straps were attached at all four corners. She would never have the strength to tear them off. He'd made sure of it.

Hearing a soft moan, he smiled. They were almost at the house. He could shock her again to ensure his safety until she was bound.

Such pleasure awaited him. Maybe he would record the two of them together and send it to Black to torment him. She would please him, of that he was certain. The more she begged, the more he would enjoy it, her words adding gas to an already unchecked fire. Ultimately, she would join the others in the morgue, but, first, she would pay the ultimate penalty for all of the arrogant bitches who had ignored him.

****

Trying to relax at home made Elijah grit his teeth. He just wanted this case to be slammed into a file drawer and marked solved. Using Dayle as bait went against everything he believed in. Especially now. Because lately, he'd been thinking about making her a permanent part of his life.

He wasn't sure whether she would ever consider marrying again. She still said little about her first marriage, but he knew from the scar it had been bad. Still, he wondered if she would be willing to move in with him. They spent so much time together anyway, and she never bored him. As soon as this craziness was over, he would give it more serious thought and come up with a plan. He always worked better with a plan.

For now, he switched on the news and tried to focus on tomorrow's scheme.

****

When Jones opened the car door, the hinges squealed in warning. She recognized him at once, peeking out from under the tarp. The fact that the killer was a cop stunned her. He'd been hiding right under their noses. But why hadn't he shot her? Using a taser was a change in modus operandi. There had been no sign of it with the other victims. Not that she wasn't grateful, but why wasn't she already dead?

Reaching in, he lifted the tarp away. She kicked him in the chest as best she could from her awkward position, knocking him back a step. "Bitch," he growled, grabbing her ankles to jerk her forward as she struggled to sit up. The stun gun appeared in his hand. She tried to reverse direction and scramble away to no avail. The arcing pain in her thigh scrambled her thoughts, and she sucked in a ragged breath. Now, her muscles were useless once again. Grinning in triumph, he pulled her out and hoisted her over his shoulder in a fireman's carry.

She tried to see as much as she could, dangling down over his back, but the inky darkness hindered her. She could see enough to know they were in a residential neighborhood. The peaked arch of Victorian architecture showed briefly before the door closed with a bang behind them.

Thinking of Elijah, she hoped he wouldn't blame himself if she didn't survive. They had no suspicions it was a cop and, by the time they figured it out, they might be too late to save her. She couldn't afford to let terror take over. *Think. Look for any opportunity to defeat him.*

He went down a hall past what looked like a living room. The few pieces of furniture and a television she could see were coated with dust. The entire house had a stale, musty odor as if it had been abandoned. She couldn't see much more until he threw her down on a bed in an adjacent room. Jouncing on the mattress made her stomach roil. "Home, sweet home," Jones jeered, laughing, as he stood braced beside her. "Not exactly what you're used to, princess."

She took a slow breath, trying to calm her nausea. Forcing the words out, she said, "Actually, I grew up in a house very like this one." It wasn't true, but she didn't want to show fear. Talking might buy her some time. Time might mean life instead of death.

He yanked her arms out from her sides, one at a time, and strapped her into place. Her arms and legs stretched open like a sacrifice, causing a horrifying vulnerability. "Please," she whispered.

"Shut up." The thick leather cuffs he buckled on dug painfully into her wrists. Continuing with her ankles, he said, "We're going to have some fun, you and me. How's your boyfriend going to like that?"

She strained to keep her voice calm. "Why are you doing this?"

The scathing sound he uttered made a mockery of laughter. "Because I'm tired of you bitches thinking you run the show. You don't. Women are put on the earth to serve man."

Memories of her husband invaded. He'd said almost identical words right before he shoved the knife in her stomach. She struggled to guess what kind of response would buy her some precious time. "Maybe you just haven't met the right woman yet."

He turned to leer at her, his gaze running down her body. "When I'm finished, every single one of you will understand your place in this world." Now he touched her, running a hand down her thigh as she struggled not to vomit. "You gave it up for that ass kisser, Black. Did he ask pretty please before he screwed you?"

"No." She met his gaze. "He knows how to treat a woman with respect, though. Do you?"

"Respect?" He gave a hoarse laugh. "We respect you, and you take our money, our jobs, then just find another man to hump."

Intuition forced her next question. "Is that what your wife did to you?" It was her best guess and she held her breath, hoping her words didn't make things worse.

Instead, he glared at her and, turning, stormed out of the room. She took the time to scan as much as she could see of the interior. There was only the one door. It looked as if another one had been boarded up with broad planks of wood nailed to the wall. She twisted, arching her back, to peer in the other direction. Two large windows had been reinforced with metal grates both inside and out. Spider webs stretched across two ceiling corners of the room. There was no attic access from here—nowhere to hide even if she managed to break free.

Dayle heard the clink of glass bottles from the other room and forced herself to concentrate. She hoped he drank some alcohol. If he drank enough, it might incapacitate him in several ways, but she couldn't count on it. Studying her sturdy restraints, she considered. The four cuffs were leather, thick and rigid, but one hadn't been attached quite as tightly as the others. She started to work on it, twisting her wrist back and forth. If she smashed her thumb, would that allow her enough room to slide free of that one cuff? One hand could free the others and…

With little warning, he reentered the room, a bottle of beer in his hand. Scoffing at her efforts, he said, "You think you're smarter than me, don't ya?"

If he was expecting a fearful response, he wouldn't get it from her. She knew from experience that begging would both engage him further and feed his arrogance. "I don't know you, so how could I possibly determine that?"

"Well, let me save you some time. You're not. And you're never going to escape this house. Not alive, anyway." He snickered and took another swig. "We'll see if Black still wants you when I'm finished with you. The stupid bastard doesn't have a clue that the infamous Rhymester has been standing right next to him the whole time."

"What did Elijah ever do to you?"

He gritted his teeth so hard, she heard the subtle scrape. "The boss gives him credit for everything in our department. I've been a detective for longer than him. Bastard thinks he's such a hotshot." Strolling over to stand beside her, he leaned over, stroking her breast. His demented gaze gleamed. "You're going to pay for that, too."

She looked away in disgust.

"Don't you turn away from me," he yelled, pulling her hair to force her to look at him. "You can't do anything without my say so. Don't friggin' breathe without my permission."

Keeping silent was her only safe recourse. And, then, something occurred to her. He'd have to remove her restraints if he wanted her clothes off. She'd have a chance. Hope plummeted seconds later when she realized he could easily cut them off.

"That's right. Keep your mouth shut." Now, his eyes heated. "Why don't I trickle this all over you and lick it up?" Reaching over, he tore her blouse open and stared at her breasts as if transfixed. The silence as he did so chilled her blood.

Panic shuddered through her. She watched, her heart thudding in her chest, as he polished off the rest of his beer and left the room. Thinking he would return immediately, she was surprised when she heard the sound of the television.

What the hell is he doing?

She shouldn't care. All that mattered is that she had some time before... She pushed the possibilities out of her mind. None of them were encouraging. Salvation may not be coming, so she had to try to save herself. When the television volume became louder, she slammed her thumb against the hefty wooden bed frame. Agony almost had her cry out loud, but she sucked in the pain, biting her lip. She whacked her thumb twice more as hard as she could. The final time she felt a decisive snap.

Breathing through her mouth, she worked through

the wrenching pain. That pain would amplify a thousandfold if she couldn't escape. As she lay there, struggling not to cry, she recognized panting sounds from the other room.

Porn. He was watching porn. Keep watching, you deviant prick, she thought, and tried to wiggle her hand free of the cuff. Every movement caused her hand to throb. At first, release seemed impossible, but she turned to find another angle. Finally, her wrist slid farther down the cuff. In a minute, she'd wrestled free and stared at her mangled hand in disbelief. Forcing her tears away, she began to work at the second cuff with the four working fingers that remained.

****

Elijah arrived at the office early and started running all of the details of tonight's operation for what seemed like the hundredth time. Around eight, he texted good morning to Dayle. She didn't answer, so he figured she must be up to her neck in files, trying to get the latter part of the day clear for their operation. By the time Sanchez arrived, he had learned that Jones had called in sick. They would have to replace him, but that would be simple enough. Other than that, everything seemed to be on track.

At nine, he and Sanchez had just reviewed some case details when the phone rang. Dayle's boss was on the other end, enquiring whether she had shown up to discuss the case with them. "No, but she's expected at three for a meeting," he replied. His shoulders tightened when the other man said she hadn't shown up for an early meeting at her office this morning. "I see. Has anyone checked her apartment?" When he replied in the negative, Elijah said that he would do so immediately and get back to him. Forewarning tensed his jaw. She wasn't the type to take time off without alerting someone.

Guilt rained down on his shoulders. Should he have called her when she didn't reply to his earlier text? He grabbed his jacket, explaining to Sanchez on the run. She scurried to keep pace with him. "I'm sure she's okay. Maybe she just slept in." He thought it unlikely and didn't bother to respond, his mind taking frightening leaps. Intuition warned him of a greater threat.

The trip over proved nerve-wracking as they ran late yellow traffic lights and zipped from lane to lane. When they arrived at her complex, they abandoned the car at the door, their permit in clear view. Hearing their concerns after checking their badges, the doorman accompanied them upstairs and let them inside for a welfare check. He called out as they opened the door, but the silence deafened him. Nothing appeared out of place in the pristine apartment, but she wasn't anywhere to be found. When he saw the bed was still unmade, her fresh nightie laid over it in preparation, he stopped, panicked now. "She didn't make it home last night."

Sanchez glanced around. "How can you be sure?"

"She told me she never makes her bed in the morning. She tidies it when she gets home after work and lays out her clothes for the next day."

"Let's not panic. Maybe last night was an exception."

He prowled some more, searching in the bathroom. He grasped the towels. "She showers in the morning, and these are bone dry."

Returning to the living room, he called her boss. "Something's wrong. It appears that she didn't make it home last night. We'll start searching for her immediately. I'll keep you informed."

Chapter Seventeen

Elijah asked the security team at her apartment to check the recordings from last night. Scrolling through, they could find no sign of Dayle arriving home from work. After determining there was nothing more to be discovered at the apartment, they returned to the precinct to marshal the resources to find her. Sanchez drove because he wasn't sure he could trust his concentration enough to stay on the road.

Hurrying up the precinct stairs to their office, they sat down at their desks and got to work. Sanchez checked the security on their building from last night and found something. The footage showed Dayle going down the front steps and, as she stepped out of the frame, black-clad arms reached out and grabbed her. Trying to prove the identity of the assailant would prove futile, but at least the evidence gave them a solid timeframe with which to work. He showed his partner. "Damn it! We can't see his face."

"True, but maybe we can find something on other cameras farther down the street." As he rallied some troops to start looking for her, one of their favorite sketch artists came to the door.

Distracted, Elijah said, "Sanchez, can you take that?"

He heard her assent and focused on who to call next. Had their killer taken Dayle? If so, why and where? Struggling to stay focused, he prayed they would be on time. A lost hour might be the difference between life and death.

"Elijah." She waved a folder to catch his attention.

He shook his head. "Just take care of it. I need to figure this out."

"No," she insisted, stamping her foot for good measure. He stared at her, surprised at her vehement tone. "You need to look at this right now."

He hurried across the room, grabbing the paper she held, ignoring the wary expression on the artist's face. "Look familiar?" Sanchez said, swearing under her breath.

Shock almost stopped his heart. It was Detective Jones. Looking up again, he stared at the artist. "How sure are you that this is accurate?"

"Pretty sure, Detective. The witness had a really good memory, better than most. He even remembered the mole he has, right by his nose." He gulped, looking from one to the other. "This is why I rushed it to you guys. I recognized him right away."

"Okay. Say nothing about this to anyone. Thank you for the excellent work."

As the man scurried off, Elijah turned to his partner. "I have to inform the lieutenant. Do a deep dive on Jones. Find out if anything in his life has changed recently to incite this."

Sanchez frowned. "I heard he just got divorced a few months ago."

"I didn't know that. Find out why they split up if you can. See if his partner knows anything else that might help. If you can get a hold of the ex-wife, see what she has to say about his current behavior."

He hurried down the crowded hall, finding his boss in a meeting with someone he didn't recognize. Porter looked up, raising an eyebrow. "Can it wait, Detective?"

"I'm afraid not, sir. It's extremely urgent." The other man left quickly, curiosity peaking his brow. Elijah closed the door behind him.

"Do you have a break in the case?"

"Yes, sir. A major one, but it will need careful handling, I'm afraid." He filled him in on Dayle's disappearance and their information about Jones.

He froze, his mouth agape. "Please tell me this is a joke."

"I'm afraid not. I wish it was. We've searched her apartment. It's clear from the security footage she never made it home last night, so her hours since leaving work around nine are unaccounted for." He paused, trying to organize his thoughts. "Sanchez is doing a search on Jones as we speak and talking to his partner and ex-wife. Missing persons has been alerted about Dayle, and we've issued a warning to be on the lookout for both of them."

He cradled his head in his hands. "Why would Jones abduct her?"

"According to Sanchez, he went through a divorce recently. It likely has something to do with that. The sketch is much better than average, though. I don't think there's any chance of error."

"Why didn't we catch this before now?"

"The witness was on a business trip. He just returned yesterday. The artist brought me the sketch as soon as they were finished."

"I assume you swore him to secrecy."

"Of course. How do you want to proceed?"

Frowning, he replied, "I think we need to have our media person apprised of what's likely coming in the near future. She'll need to protect the integrity of the department after this gets out. Pamela Clayton might be willing to help us spin the story when the time comes." He met Elijah's gaze. "And you? I know you and Dayle have a relationship. Are you capable of leading this search?"

"Yes, sir. I'll find her." He forced the words out, praying he could. "I'll find them both."

Thirty minutes later, armed with a warrant, they gained entry to Jones's home. The small apartment wasn't far from the precinct. Elijah paused just inside the shabby door, assessing the depressing interior. The whole place reeked of alcohol and cheap aftershave. Plain beige walls framed the tiny living room and kitchen. Empty beer bottles sat clustered on the stained coffee table. Fast food refuse had toppled onto the floor. He let the others search those rooms as he headed for the bedroom. What he found there raised the hair on his arms.

Cut out photographs of women coated the inside of the closet as well as the doors which had been left flung open. His clothes hung in a bunched fashion on the lower rod. The top portion revealed even more disturbing pictures. On closer look, he found darts lying on the shelf. Peering at the photographs themselves, he saw dart holes and, over some, the word, 'bitch,' spelled out in bleeding red marker.

He examined some of the faces more closely. All three victims were there with a big check mark over their faces. Sanchez and Clayton were in a corner with

'To be continued' noted beside the print. Mrs. King was there, too, with a circle around her face.

His phone rang, and he saw it was Sanchez. When he answered, she said, "I found something interesting. Eighteen months ago, Jones inherited an old Victorian house from his stepfather. It's a dive, been sitting on the market for eighteen months."

"They might be there."

"My best guess at this point. I'm sending you the address now."

"Call SWAT. Make sure they know who Dayle is so we get priority. I'll meet them there."

"I'll call them and head over, too."

"Good. Meet you there in twenty." He left two officers to be in charge of processing the evidence and ran to his car. Tapping the address Sanchez had given him into the GPS, he sped away. If SWAT couldn't arrive on time, he planned to go in, no matter what happened. Using his siren to alert traffic as he sped through lights, he prayed that if she was there, she'd found a way to survive and could hold on just a little longer.

****

Dayle hadn't heard anything from Jones in a long while. She had freed her arms and one leg, stretched them to regain feeling, then started on her second leg. If he caught her, he would likely kill her, but she had no choice. She couldn't let him win.

Whenever she heard a sound, she pushed her joints back under the flaps so he couldn't tell she'd freed herself. When she finally got her second ankle free, she almost sobbed with relief. *But, what now?* She could tell from the earlier sounds that he sat very close to the door. She'd never make it over a squeaky old wooden floor to make it to the door.

Her only chance would be to catch him by surprise and overpower him. Was there a back door? Probably, but the time wasted in finding it could be fatal.

Suddenly, a rustling sound had her holding her breath.

Oh, no. Is he waking up?

For the first time in years, she prayed.

****

Sanchez pulled in right behind Elijah and slipped out of her borrowed car into theirs. Huddled in the passenger seat, she turned to face him. "Porter is on his way, but SWAT is still fifteen minutes away stuck in traffic. "What do you want to do? Your call."

They couldn't afford to wait. Dayle might not have that long if she was still alive. "Watch the front," he told his partner. "I'll check it out and report back."

"Be careful."

He slipped along beside the trees, hoping the shadows of a gray, drizzly day would shield him. The spacious front rooms appeared to be empty, but he came to a room on the side that had reinforced windows. Putting his ear against them, he could hear a murmur of a woman's voice. He couldn't tell if it was Dayle. Suddenly, a man's raised voice could be heard, and it sounded like Jones. He heard the word bitch and not much else, but the threatening tenor of his words gave them no choice.

Trying to stay out of view, he slipped back to the car. Another pair of detectives had pulled to the curb behind them. He told them to watch the front, he intended to find a way in. When he tried to convince

Sanchez to wait for SWAT, she said, "Give me a break. I'll cover your bony ass like I always do."

Not bothering to argue, he explained the layout and about the room where he thought she was being held. "Okay, let's go." They stole their way to the front door, standing on either side in case he'd seen them coming. Elijah rested his hand on the cold metal knob and turned, surprised to find it unlocked. He nodded to Sanchez. Easing the door open, he went high, she covered low, sweeping their guns in a predictable arc to check the corners of the room. Jones's voice could be heard, still elevated in anger. He heard Dayle murmur a response, and relief rushed through him, weakening his knees.

But she wasn't safe yet.

They quietly stepped forward through the living area to the open door of the room where shadows played against the wall. A figure on the far wall was clearly Jones, his arms gesturing, the outline of his pistol clear. A shape beyond appeared to be a bed with Dayle's body secured somehow to hefty posts. Elijah needed to get that gun pointed at him, not her. Advancing slowly, he almost made it through the doorway when a wooden board creaked beneath his feet.

Jones whirled toward him, shock causing his jaw to drop. Pointing his gun, he squeezed off a shot, then lunged toward the bed. Elijah fired, hitting his leg. Dayle suddenly yanked free, diving off the other side of the large bed to the floor. His target out of reach, Jones swung his gun in their direction. He and Sanchez both fired, the sound an assault of its own in the small room. Jones, his face a caricature of surprise, tumbled to the floor. Sanchez leapt to restrain him, kicking his gun away.

When he was certain all was secure, Elijah hurried to where Dayle lay, bruised and trembling against the wall. "Are you okay?" He squatted down beside her, his eyes raking her body for injuries.

"I am n-now," she stuttered, trying to cover herself.

"Stand down," he said into his radio. "Subject is down and in custody." He took his jacket off and handed it to Dayle, helping her on with it. Her shaking slowed her actions, and she winced as she slid one arm in. "What did you hurt?" Closing his arms around Dayle, he heard the sounds of other officers enter. "Back here," he called. He turned to repeat his question. "What did you hurt?"

She offered a wan smile. "I had to smash one thumb to get out of my cuffs."

Leaning over, he peered at it, wincing. Red and swollen to twice its size, the thumb dangled to one side. "I wondered how you got free. You made quite a swan dive. Good reflexes." As his heart finally settled, he raised her carefully to her feet, supporting her under her arms. He wrapped his arm around her for support, wanting to sweep her into his arms, but knowing she wanted to exit on her own two feet. "Come on. We'll get the EMTs to take care of you." He paused to check with Sanchez. She shook her head, confirming Jones was deceased.

"What about him?" Dayle gestured toward the body, shivering.

"Don't worry. He's never going to hurt anyone again." He kissed her cheek, and they made their way to the front door where their lieutenant stood. Looking up, he shook his head, and the other man followed them outside. As Dayle was getting taken care of, he filled him in on what had happened inside the house.

"You and Sanchez both shot him?"

"Yes, sir. At the same time. Both impacted."

"Anything unusual about those final moments I need to know about?"

"No, sir. He fired first, and I shot him in the leg. After Dayle dove out of the way, he swung toward us in firing position and squeezed off a second round. We had no choice."

He rubbed his face, looking exhausted. "Just between you and me, it's for the best. A messy trial and a death sentence would be an even bigger black eye for the department."

"Yes, sir." Others may not appreciate such a frank assessment, but he did. He handed the other man his gun and watched as Sanchez did the same.

Porter stood looking at the two black vans parked nearby that had a cluster of men in attack gear standing by. "The SWAT commander wasn't happy you didn't wait, but I'll handle him. Good work, you two."

He and a few SWAT officers hadn't been the best of friends since the Cara Belton case. "Thank you, sir."

The two of them rejoined Dayle who'd been bandaged up. "They want me to go to the hospital and have this splinted." She grimaced. "Apparently, I did a real number on it."

"Do you have much pain?"

"They gave me something to help. It's not bad."

He knew she'd never admit it hurt a lot. He stroked her hair, then stood back as the ambulance driver prepared to shut the doors. "I'll see Sanchez off and meet you there."

While his partner got started on the lengthy report generated by the incident, he sat in a hospital waiting room. When Dayle re-emerged, she had a short, molded splint on her hand and wrist. "The doctor told me I should be more careful. I told him I really hadn't anticipated being kidnapped by a crazed serial killer."

"Shame on you," he teased. Taking her arm, he started for the door. "I'll make you a deal. Come back to the precinct long enough to give us your statement. When we're finished, we'll dope you up with pain pills, call Ray, and have a celebratory dinner somewhere."

"And then?"

"Then let's go home so I can pamper you a little bit."

She quirked an eyebrow. "Just a little bit?"

"Maybe a lot."

"Now, that sounds like the best plan I've heard all day."

He'd forgotten about the throng of reporters clustered around the entrance. Cursing himself for not taking her out the back door, he put his arm around Dayle and hustled her through the crowd as best he could. He opened the passenger door and helped her with her seatbelt. "Is she your girlfriend?" a voice yelled and, frowning, he answered, "No comment."

Taking his seat behind the wheel, he belted up, then honked the horn to warn them he was going to move. They took a few reluctant steps back, trying to peek through the windows for a better look. He eased out onto the street, ignoring the shouts of protest, and drove away.

She laughed. "Am I your girlfriend?"

"It's such a moronic term at our age, isn't it?"

'Yes. I prefer lover myself. It's sexy."

"I agree." He leaned over to squeeze her good hand.

"Happy this case is finally over?"

He nodded. "I'm especially grateful that you're safe and we didn't have to call in the FBI."

Writing the reports and taking the necessary statements took a few hours. Afterwards, the lieutenant and the district attorney gave them the rest of the day off to celebrate. They arranged to meet the others at Ray's favorite restaurant, an Italian trattoria owned by one of his aunts.

In the meantime, they went to Dayle's, and he waited while she packed an overnight bag. Back at Elijah's, they both showered and changed into casual clothes. "Sanchez asked me if I ever wore anything besides beige and black," she said, pointing at her new blue skirt and lavender blouse. "She might have a point."

He shrugged. "You always look beautiful to me."

"Looking to score some lover points?" she asked, raising an eyebrow.

"If I manage to do that, can I cash them in later?"

"I'm counting on it."

When they arrived, Ray and Sanchez were already there, huge glasses of sangria in their hands. They waved them to a big table in the center of the room and poured them glasses as well. A soulful song poured from the speakers as Ray introduced his aunt, a short, curvy woman, her hair wound in a neat braided bun. Aunt Rosa hugged them all, flirting a little with Elijah. She shook her head, smiling at Dayle, said something they couldn't translate and scurried away.

"I don't speak Italian." Dayle waited for Ray to explain.

"She said you're too skinny. Said she'd soon take care of that." He smiled. "She means no harm. It's just her way."

They laughed and sat. Sanchez held her drink up in a toast. "Here's to a little peace and quiet before the next one comes along. And to Dayle's ten-point dive off the bed to save her ass."

"Cheers to that," Elijah said, clinking glasses with the others. They chatted for just a few minutes before platters of food came. Homemade lasagna of three different kinds sat next to two baskets of crusty bread. One huge jug of sangria got swapped for another fresh one.

Well into the meal, Dayle leaned over to Sanchez. Catching Elijah's eye, she said, "So, what revealing stories can you tell me about him?" Chuckling, he waited to see what his partner would share.

She rubbed her hands together, a mischievous look stretching her grin. "Oooh, the embarrassing things I could tell you." Suddenly, her face sobered. "Seriously, here's the honest truth." Shocked to see tears in her eyes, he listened closely. "He's the best partner a chica like me could ever ask for. Besides my guy"—she reached to grab Ray's hand—"he's the best man you'll ever meet."

Meeting her gaze, he said, "Thanks, partner."

She rolled her eyes and used her napkin to wipe the damp trails from her face. "Don't get all fat-headed on me. I'll probably change my mind tomorrow."

"That's fair," he replied.

They all dug in to finish their food. Elijah smiled as he ate, pondering the idea that the perfect family picture looked different to everyone. His clan just happened to be part Hispanic, part Italian, and now included a tall, brainy woman who might just be his forever girl. He knew his parents would tell him to grab hold and cherish that for the rest of his life. As always, he would take their advice and run with it.

Epilogue

Later that night, Sanchez perched on the edge of the porcelain bathtub in her apartment. The traffic noise from the street below played a familiar, melodic tune that kept her company. Ray had fallen asleep wrapped around her almost an hour ago. She had wiggled out from underneath his heavy arm and come to do her private errand in secret.

She had her suspicions, but she needed to be certain. The white shaped stick sat on the melamine countertop as she monitored the minutes on her watch to keep time.

Taking a breath and reaching for it, she checked the small square window. Sure enough, the colored line that waited there confirmed what she expected. Her hand shook as she set the stick back down. A rush of unexpected joy took hold of her and shook her to her core. But, then, a moment of doubt intervened. What the hell did she know about being a good mother?

It didn't matter. She could learn. Her friends would help. Hell, Elijah probably knew a million weird facts about babies.

Now, how to tell Ray?

As if the thought had conjured him up, a knock came on the door. The sleepy sound of his husky baritone reached her ears. "You okay, babe?"

"Yup, I'm coming." Taking a deep breath, she opened the door.

A word about the author…

Dianne McCartney has been writing for seventeen years and has won sixty-three writing awards in contests across Texas and Oklahoma. She is a long-standing member of the Oklahoma Writers Federation, Inc. and a proud member of the Rose Rock Writers.

Website:
www.diannemccartney.com

Social Media Links:
https://twitter.com/authorDMcC
https://www.facebook.com/dianne.mccartney.3914/
https://www.instagram.com/diannemccartney1200
https://www.linkedin.com/in/dianne-mccartney-36a493161/